# STRATEGIES FOR TEACHING

## Technology

D1448839

MENC wishes to thank
Carolynn A. Lindeman for developing and coordinating this series;
*Sam Reese, Kimberly McCord,* and *Kimberly Walls* for selecting, writing, and editing the
strategies for this book;
and the following teachers for submitting strategies:

| | | |
|---|---|---|
| Cecil Adderley | Tammy Gould | William Pardus |
| Lorraine Arcari | Sara Hagen | Sondra Paulson |
| Stephan Barnicle | Wendy Hinshaw Hefner | Valerie Peters |
| William Bauer | Caroline Hensley | Heike Petith |
| Todd Beaney | John Jinright | Beth Pickard |
| Betsy Bergeron | Brian Kabat | Polly Sibert |
| Patricia Bissell | Kirk Kassner | Jacqueline Cratin Smith |
| Jeffrey E. Bush | Judy Krugman | David Snyder |
| Richard Dammers | Janice Lancaster | Wayne Splettstoeszer |
| Dina Dorough | Anna Larsen | Jay Stoltzfus |
| David Ferguson | Dennis Mauricio | Jill von Trebra |
| Laura Ferguson | Naomi Mellendorf | Lee Walkup |
| Margaret Fitzgerald | Jason Meltzer | Scott Watson |
| James T. Frankel | Charles Menoche | Sherrie Welles |
| Debra Gordon | Paula Nelson | Rachel Whitcomb |

# STRATEGIES FOR TEACHING

## Technology

*Compiled and edited*

by Sam Reese, Kimberly McCord, and Kimberly Walls

YOUR KEY TO
IMPLEMENTING
THE NATIONAL
STANDARDS
FOR MUSIC
EDUCATION

MENC—THE NATIONAL ASSOCIATION FOR MUSIC EDUCATION

· Series Editor: Carolynn A. Lindeman

Project Administrator: Margaret A. Senko

Copyright © 2001
MENC—The National Association for Music Education
1806 Robert Fulton Drive
Reston, VA 20191

# CONTENTS

# PREFACE

MENC—The National Association for Music Education (formerly the Music Educators National Conference) created the *Strategies for Teaching* series to help preservice and in-service music educators implement the K–12 National Standards for Music Education and the MENC Prekindergarten Standards. To address the many components of the school music curriculum, each book in the series focuses on a specific curricular area and a particular level. The result is twelve books spanning the K–12 areas of band, chorus, general music, strings/orchestra, guitar, keyboard, and specialized ensembles. A prekindergarten book and a guide for college music methods classes complete the series.

The purpose of the series is to seize the opportunity presented by the landmark education legislation of 1994. With the passage of the Goals 2000: Educate America Act, the arts were established for the first time in our country's history as a core, challenging subject in which all students need to demonstrate competence. Voluntary academic standards were called for in all nine of the identified core subjects—standards specifying what students need to know and be able to do when they exit grades 4, 8, and 12.

In music, content and achievement standards were drafted by an MENC task force. They were examined and commented on by music teachers across the country, and the task force reviewed their comments and refined the standards. While all students in grades K–8 are expected to meet the achievement standards specified for those levels, two levels of achievement—proficient and advanced—are designated for students in grades 9–12. Students who elect music courses for one to two years beyond grade 8 are expected to perform at the proficient level. Students who elect music courses for three to four years beyond grade 8 are expected to perform at the advanced level.

The music standards, together with the dance, theatre, and visual arts standards, were presented in final form—*National Standards for Arts Education*—to the U.S. Secretary of Education in March 1994. Recognizing the importance of early childhood education, MENC went beyond the K–12 standards and established content and achievement standards for the prekindergarten level as well, which are included in MENC's *The School Music Program: A New Vision.*

Now the challenge at hand is to implement the standards at the state and local levels. Implementation may require schools to expand the resources necessary to achieve the standards as specified in MENC's *Opportunity-to-Learn Standards for Music Instruction: Grades PreK–12.* Teachers will need to examine their curricula to determine if they lead to achievement of the standards. For many, the standards reflect exactly what has always been included in the school music curriculum—they represent best practice. For others, the standards may call for some curricular expansion.

To assist in the implementation process, this series offers teaching strategies illustrating how the music standards can be put into action in the music classroom. The strategies themselves do not suggest a curriculum. That, of course, is the responsibility of school districts and individual teachers. The strategies, however, are designed to help in curriculum development, lesson planning, and assessment of music learning.

The teaching strategies are based on the content and achievement standards specified in the *National Standards for Arts Education* (K–12) and *The School Music Program: A New Vision* (PreK–12). Although the strategies, like the standards, are designed primarily for four-year-olds, fourth graders, eighth graders, and high school seniors, many may be developmentally appropriate for students in other grades. Each strategy, a lesson appropriate for a portion of a class session or a complete class session, includes an objective (a clear statement of what the student will be able to do), a list of necessary materials, a description of what prior student learning and experiences are expected, a set of procedures, and the indicators of success. A follow-up section identifies ways learning may be expanded.

The *Guide for Music Methods Classes* contains strategies appropriate for preservice instructional settings in choral, instrumental, and general music methods classes. The teaching strategies in this guide relate to the other books in the series and reflect a variety of teaching/learning styles.

Bringing a series of fourteen books from vision to reality in a little over a year's time required tremendous commitment from many, many music educators—not to mention the tireless help of the MENC publications staff. Literally hundreds of music teachers across the country answered the call to participate in this project, the largest such participation in an MENC publishing endeavor. The contributions of these teachers and the books' editors are proudly presented in the various publications.

—*Carolynn A. Lindeman*
Series Editor

*Carolynn A. Lindeman, professor of music at San Francisco State University, served on the MENC task force that developed the music education standards. She is the author of three college textbooks* (The Musical Classroom, PianoLab, *and* MusicLab) *and numerous articles.*

# INTRODUCTION

During the 1990s, many Americans became infatuated with computer and networking technologies. These powerful technologies increasingly pervaded our lives and began changing substantially the way we work, learn, communicate, and entertain ourselves. A recent national poll reports, "Americans … overwhelmingly think that computers and the Internet have made Americans' lives better. … Enthusiasm for computers and the Internet runs wide and deep, across all incomes, all regions of the country, all races, all political ideologies, and most age groups."[1] In spite of concerns over inappropriate content, invasion of privacy, and inequality of access to technology, almost nine out of ten (87%) Americans under the age of sixty say computers have made life better for them, and more than seven out of ten (72%) say the Internet has made life better. In addition, more than two-thirds (68%) of working Americans use a computer at work, and 84% of them say it is essential for their jobs.

Children ages 10–17 are even more eager about these technologies. Nearly all have access to computers at school, and 63% of their classrooms have Internet access.[2] Almost eight out of ten (78%) have a computer at home. Of these, 57% use the computer every day, with 88% using it to do school work and 73% having access to the Internet.

In the midst of this zeal for technology, the need for this book is clear. It provides music educators with practical teaching strategies for using computer, networking, and music technologies to help students achieve the National Standards. It was prepared in direct response to the call from the MENC Technology Task Force to help teachers focus on applying technology to the music classroom through exemplars, models, and lesson plans. In support of the MENC Opportunity-to-Learn Technology Standards, it gives detail and depth to the standards in that document related to curriculum and scheduling, staffing, equipment, materials and software, and facilities.

Even in the face of many challenges to technology use in schools, imaginative music educators across America have found numerous ways to use technology in their teaching. They not only use computers to do the many administrative and communication tasks they face, but they also are preparing stimulating teaching materials, leading engaging classroom activities, and involving students in direct, hands-on uses of computers for music learning. Recent studies have

# HARDWARE AND SOFTWARE EXPLANATIONS

## Computer-Related Hardware

The amount and type of computer-related hardware needed varies considerably among the strategies. The following list provides further explanation of items that may be called for in the Materials sections of the strategies:

- *Computer*—Unless specified, this can be either a Macintosh or Windows (IBM-PC) computer. The processing (CPU) speed, memory (RAM), and storage space (hard drive size) needed vary considerably among the strategies. In many cases older computers will be sufficient, but other strategies will require newer computers with higher specifications.

- *General MIDI sound generation*—This refers to the ability of the workstation to play sound generated by MIDI music software. This is accomplished by either (1) use of the internal sound generation of the computer (internal sound card—Windows; QuickTime Musical Instruments—Macintosh); or (2) connecting the computers to General MIDI keyboards using a MIDI interface. When the strategy calls only for playback of software files, the internal sound generation is sufficient. However, when the strategy calls for students to play or record from a keyboard or other MIDI instrument, then the General MIDI keyboard is needed.

- *CD- or DVD-ROM drive*—A drive for using CD-ROM software or for playing audio CDs. DVD-ROM drives will play all CD-ROM software and audio CDs.

- *Powered speakers or headphones*—The sound from the computer and/or the keyboard must be amplified to be heard. The sound-out jack of the computer and/or keyboard must be connected to powered speakers or headphones. The sound-out jack of computers and keyboards can be connected to most classroom stereos so that it can be amplified for groups to hear. If both the sound of the computer and the sound of the keyboard must be heard simultaneously (as when using sequencing software with digital audio), a simple audio mixer will be needed in most cases.

- *Internet access*—The computer will need to be connected to the Internet, either through a dedicated network connection or a modem connection.

- *Computer display projector*—These devices allow larger groups to see the screen being displayed on the computer monitor. This is usually done by connecting the video-out of the computer to (1) a large-screen TV using a scan converter box, (2) an LCD panel on an overhead projector, or (3) an LCD projector.

- *Microphone*—Some computers have internal, "built-in" microphones. Others need to have an external microphone connected to the sound-in jack of the computer. Strategies that call for microphones can be completed with basic level microphones.

- *Video-in capability*—The computer will need to have a digital video card, which can digitize the video output of video cameras, or VCRs. The video output from cameras or VCRs can be connected by NTSC (composite) video or by S-video. NTSC video output is available on all video equipment and uses RCA-style connectors, like those commonly used in stereo equipment.

- *CD-ROM burner*—A CD-ROM drive that can write (burn) software files onto CD-R disks.

## Configuring Software for Sound

Many titles of current MIDI music software can be configured to play sound using the internal General MIDI sound generation capability of the computer or by connecting to a MIDI keyboard or sound module. When the strategy does not call for MIDI keyboards, the software may be configured to use the internal General MIDI sound generation. On Windows computers, use the internal sound card. On Macintosh computers, have the QuickTime Musical Instruments system software installed. The documentation that comes with MIDI software explains how to make the correct settings for using internal General MIDI sound generation.

shown that more than 75% of music teachers use technology for some aspect of their jobs and that over 90% of practicing music teachers would like to have additional training in the use of technology.[3]

Much work remains to be done, however, before large numbers of students can benefit from learning music with technology. Currently, less than 30% of practicing K–12 music teachers are able to use computers during actual instruction with students, due not only to restricted access to technology but also to limited availability of technology training for teachers. In Illinois, for example, only 13% of school districts offer music technology training once a year, and only 25% of teachers have received formal technology training at a university.[4]

This book can partially help address some of these needs. It provides a diverse range of strategies that were developed by an enthusiastic group of music teachers from many states in response to the MENC call for teaching strategies that use technology. The strategies provide "real-world" approaches to infusing technology into music classrooms and rehearsal rooms and help reduce some of the complexities and mysteries surrounding the use of technology. They place technology in its proper role of being a means to achieving important music learning goals and avoid a technocentric orientation of using technology for its own sake. The strategies range from simple to complex— from word processing to using e-mail listservs and software used for computer-assisted instruction, MIDI-based notation, sequencing, accompaniment and digital audio recording, presentation, and multimedia, as well as other software. The strategies also reflect the diversity of levels of access to technology that teachers face—from only a personal computer at home to one in the classroom, to two or more in the classroom, to school computer labs, up to dedicated music technology labs. Often the strategies do not describe a particular type of classroom setting, in order not to limit the adaptability of these activities to only certain levels and types of access to technology.

Whatever circumstances you may face, we encourage you to adapt these strategies to your own setting and to other grades and types of classes. Even though a strategy may have the label of middle-level general music, it might well be adapted for grades K–4. A performing ensemble strategy may be readily adapted to the use of classroom instruments in a general music classroom.

Whenever possible, the strategies are written in general language so that they are appropriate for both Macintosh and Windows computers. In the Materials section of each strategy, when the word "computer" is used, it means that either platform can be used. Likewise, software is referred to by type rather than specific titles when possible. For instance, the wording "notation software, such as *Finale* or *Encore*" is used, rather than limiting the strategy to a single notation software program. The software called for is most often available for both platforms and is readily available through school music vendors or by downloading from the World Wide Web. (See Hardware and Software Explanations on page 2 for additional information.)

When used well, computer and music technologies increase the level of thinking, learning, and engagement of our students beyond what can be done with traditional materials alone. These strategies demonstrate that technology can be a powerful tool for promoting the development of high levels of skill and understanding in musical performance, critical listening, creative thinking, and problem-solving with music.

Also, we are beginning to get glimpses of how technology can stretch the boundaries of our traditional general music and performance programs beyond the physical limits of our classrooms and rehearsal rooms. It helps bring distant resources more easily into the reach of our students and helps us reach students when they are at home or in other classrooms. At their best, these technologies may help students learn music anytime or anywhere and help us expand the limited amounts of learning time that students now have with us.

## Notes

1. National Public Radio, "Survey Shows Widespread Enthusiasm for High Technology" [online], (2000), available at http://www.npr.org/programs/specials/poll/technology/

2. U.S. Department of Education, "Internet Access in U.S. Public Schools and Classrooms: 1994–1999" [online], (2000), available at http://nces.ed.gov/pubs2000/2000086.pdf

3. Steven Hedden and Debra Gordon, "Computer Usage among K–12 Music Educators," paper presented at the Southeastern Music Education

Symposium, Athens, Georgia (May 1999); Sam Reese and James Rimington, "Music Technology in Illinois Public Schools," *Update: Applications of Research in Music Education* 18 (2), 27–32; Karin H. Sehmann and Christopher Hayes, "The Status of Computer Technology in Kentucky's Music Classrooms," poster session presented at the national convention of Music Educators National Conference, Kansas City, MO (April 1996); Jack Taylor and John Deal, "Integrating Technology into the K–12 Music Curriculum: A Pilot Survey of Music Teachers," paper presented at the Sixth International Conference on Music Education Technology, San Antonio, TX (January 1999).

4. Sam Reese and James Rimington, "Music Technology in Illinois Public Schools," *Update: Applications of Research in Music Education,* 18 (2), 27–32.

# GENERAL MUSIC
## Grades K–4

# STANDARD 1C

*Singing, alone and with others, a varied repertoire of music:* Students sing from memory a varied repertoire of songs representing genres and styles from diverse cultures.

## Objective

■ Students will sing, from memory and with correct pitches and rhythms, an accompanied unison song representing a specific genre from a specific culture.

## Materials

■ Computer with Internet access and web browser software such as *Netscape Communicator* (Mountain View, CA: Netscape) or *Internet Explorer* (Redmond, WA: Microsoft Corporation), audio-out capability, General MIDI sound generation (internal sound card—Windows; QuickTime Musical Instruments—Macintosh) connected to powered speakers or headphones

■ Computer video projector

## Other Requirements

■ Teacher search of Internet for addition of bookmarks to browser for songs, in MIDI format, representing genres from diverse cultures

## Prior Knowledge and Experiences

■ Students have experience singing songs with accompaniment.

## Procedures

1. Use the computer, speakers, and projector to display the lyrics of a selected children's song representing a particular genre or culture. Play back the associated MIDI file. If the song playback does not have a "bouncing ball," move the mouse to point to and track the lyrics.

2. Repeat step 1 while singing the song. Discuss the meaning of the lyrics and the genre or cultural background of the song.

3. Repeat step 1 while students sing one chorus of the song. Stress pitch and rhythmic accuracy.

4. Repeat step 3 until students can sing one chorus of the song from memory with accurate pitches and rhythms.

## Indicators of Success

■ Students sing the chorus from memory with correct lyrics, pitches, and rhythms.

## Follow-up

■ Use the steps under Procedures to help students learn the rest of the selected song.

# STANDARD 1D

*Singing, alone and with others, a varied repertoire of music:* Students sing ostinatos, partner songs, and rounds.

## Objective

- Students will sing a familiar song in a two-part round.

## Materials

- Computer with audio-out capability, General MIDI sound generation, and powered speakers

- Notation software such as *Finale* (Eden Prairie, MN: Coda Music Technology), *Sibelius* (Cambridge, England: The Sibelius Group), or *Encore* (Philadelphia: GVOX) [*Note:* Scrolling playback is a plus.]

- Computer video projector

- Teacher-prepared notation file with song notated on each of two staves (different color for notes on each staff) as each voice of the canon enters

## Prior Knowledge and Experiences

- Students have sung the selected song in unison.

## Procedures

1. Display the score of the selected song through the video projector, hiding staff two. Mute voice two and play the score back as the students sing the song.

2. Display and play both staves. Ask students what was different about the song. Continue playing and inquiring until students realize that the identical melody was played each time, but the voices started at different times.

3. Divide the class into two groups and have them sing the song as a two-part round while the two-voice score is played back.

4. When students are comfortable singing in two parts, have them sing the song in parts without accompaniment.

## Indicators of Success

- Students sing an unaccompanied two-part round with correct pitches and rhythm.

## Follow-up

- Divide the class into four groups. Have students sing a four-part round that you display and play.

# STANDARD 2C

*Performing on instruments, alone and with others, a varied repertoire of music:* Students perform expressively a varied repertoire of music representing diverse genres and styles.

## Objective

■ Students will play the recorder expressively in two different styles, varying the tempo, articulation, and dynamics to fit the style of the accompaniment.

## Materials

■ Computer with General MIDI sound generation (internal sound card—Windows; QuickTime Musical Instruments—Macintosh) connected to powered speakers or headphones; or computer connected to General MIDI keyboards with powered speakers or headphones

■ Accompaniment software such as *Band-in-a-Box* (Victoria, BC: PG Music) or *Visual Arranger* (Buena Vista, CA: Yamaha Corporation of America)

■ Teacher-created accompaniment software file with the chord progression appropriate for a selected song in two different accompaniment styles, with a short introduction, at appropriate tempos (optional: melody entered via the melody menu) [*Note:* Choose styles with obvious differences, such as Latin and Classical.]

## Prior Knowledge and Experiences

■ Students have at least beginning recorder-playing skills.

## Procedures

1. Have students listen to the introduction to the selected song and then play along with the first accompaniment style.

2. Change the accompaniment style and repeat step 1. Ask students for ideas about how to vary their playing to fit the two different styles (for example, playing legato vs. staccato).

3. Have the class play their part in the two styles with appropriate articulations (legato vs. staccato) and expression, as suggested by students.

4. Ask students to choose one style, and have them play their part expressively, adding appropriate dynamics.

## Indicators of Success

■ Students play the recorder expressively in two different styles, using appropriate tempo, articulation, and dynamics.

## Follow-up

■ Guide students in the process of creating a new recorder accompaniment for the song used in the Procedures, having them make choices regarding style, tempo, and instrumentation.

# STANDARD 2F

*Performing on instruments, alone and with others, a varied repertoire of music: Students perform
independent instrumental parts while other students sing or play contrasting parts.*

## Objective

- Students will perform independent parts on African percussion instruments with a teacher-generated MIDI file

## Materials

- Computer with General MIDI sound generation (internal sound card—Windows; QuickTime Musical Instruments—Macintosh) connected to powered speakers or headphones; or computer connected to General MIDI keyboards with powered speakers or headphones

- Accompaniment software such as *Band-in-a-Box* (Victoria, BC: PG Music) or *Visual Arranger* (Buena Vista, CA: Yamaha Corporation of America)

- Teacher-generated accompaniment file, using a song from *Let Your Voice Be Heard: Songs from Ghana and Zimbabwe*, 2d ed., by Abraham Kobena Adzenyah, Dumisani Maraire, and Judith Cook Tucker (Danbury, CT: World Music Press, 1997)

- Recording for *Let Your Voice Be Heard*

- African percussion instruments

- Audiocassette recorder with microphone and blank tape

## Prior Knowledge and Experiences

- Students have experience with correct playing of African percussion instruments.

## Procedures

1. Ask students to listen and identify the instruments used in the selected song from *Let Your Voice Be Heard*.

2. Teach students the percussion parts to accompany the song.

3. Ask students to play their percussion parts individually, then together as a group.

4. Have students perform the percussion parts with the accompaniment file (drum part should be muted). Record the performance.

5. Play back the recording of the student performance and ask students to evaluate their playing, comparing it to the performance on the professional recording.

## Indicators of Success

- Students independently perform on African percussion instruments with a MIDI accompaniment.

## Follow-up

- Have students perform the piece from the Procedures in a concert.

*Improvising melodies, variations, and accompaniments:* Students improvise "answers" in the same style to given rhythmic and melodic phrases.

## Objective

- Students will improvise "answers" to teacher calls over a C Jam Blues.

## Materials

- Computer with General MIDI sound generation (internal sound card—Windows; QuickTime Musical Instruments—Macintosh) connected to powered speakers or headphones; or computer connected to General MIDI keyboard with powered speakers or headphones
- Accompaniment software such as *Band-in-a-Box* (Victoria, BC: PG Music) or *Visual Arranger* (Buena Vista, CA: Yamaha Corporation of America)
- Audiocassette recorder
- Teacher-generated accompaniment software file of a C Jam Blues with a jazz swing style
- Two suspended cymbals

## Prior Knowledge and Experiences

- Students have listened to call and response—such as "Shoo, Turkey," on *Been in the Storm So Long: Spirituals, Folk Tales and Children's Games* (Smithsonian Folkways 40031) and "Rockin' the Blues," on *The Essential Count Basie, vol. 3* (Legacy/Sony Music VCK 44150).
- Students have experienced call and response in movement while moving to C Jam Blues.
- Students can properly play a suspended cymbal.

## Procedures

1. Have students practice call and response in movement with the teacher-generated MIDI file of a C Jam Blues to familiarize themselves with the music for which they will be improvising suspended cymbal responses.

2. Using the suspended cymbal, model for students playing of the jazz patterns heard in C Jam Blues. For example:

3. Play a four-bar pattern in swing style on a suspended cymbal and have one student answer with a four-bar pattern in the same style on a second suspended cymbal.

4. Using *Band-in-a-Box* C Jam Blues, have students improvise answers to the questions that you play.

## Indicators of Success

- Students improvise answers in a jazz style to teacher questions over a blues pattern.

## Follow-up

- Using the blues from the Procedures, have students play questions while other students improvise answers.
- Have students play complete twelve-bar improvised solos using jazz rhythms.

*Improvising melodies, variations, and accompaniments: Students improvise "answers" in the same style to given rhythmic and melodic phrases.*

## Objective

- Students will create "answers" to "questions" in a jazz style and record their answers using General MIDI sounds.

## Materials

- Computer with General MIDI sound generation (internal sound card—Windows; QuickTime Musical Instruments—Macintosh) connected to powered speakers or headphones; or computer connected to General MIDI keyboards with powered speakers or headphones

- *Band-in-a-Box* accompaniment software (Victoria, BC: PG Music)

- Teacher-generated four-measure accompaniment file (loaded on all stations), using *Band-in-a-Box* on a C Major triad with jazz-style rhythm section

## Prior Knowledge and Experiences

- Students can open and play *Band-in-a-Box* files.

- Students have some experience performing musical questions and answers.

## Procedures

1. Have students listen at their workstations to the four-measure MIDI accompaniment file you have created in a jazz style.

2. Ask students to display percussion instruments by clicking on the picture of a drum in the upper right-hand corner of the computer screen.

3. Have students take turns clicking on various instruments with the mouse, "trading fours" (playing four-bar phrases in turn), in order to create musical questions and answers over the MIDI accompaniment in a jazz style.

4. Have students repeat trading fours, this time clicking on the record button and recording their question and answers.

5. Ask students to play their improvisations back for the class.

## Indicators of Success

- Students improvise musical questions and answers in a jazz style.

## Follow-up

- Have students change the style from jazz to African, Latin Rock, or another style and record improvised questions and answers in the new style.

# STANDARD 3B

*Improvising melodies, variations, and accompaniments:* Students improvise simple rhythmic and melodic ostinato accompaniments.

## Objective

- Students will improvise ostinatos using rhythmic and melodic variations.

## Materials

- Computer with General MIDI sound generation (internal sound card—Windows; QuickTime Musical Instruments—Macintosh) connected to powered speakers or headphones; or computer connected to General MIDI keyboard with powered speakers or headphones
- *Band-in-a-Box* (Victoria, BC: PG Music) accompaniment software
- Teacher-generated *Band-in-a-Box* file of C Blues, using the style ZZJAZZSW.STY so that the bass part will play back in half notes on I and V (see page 16)
- Keyboard or barred instruments
- Computer display projector and screen

## Prior Knowledge and Experiences

- Students are familiar with the chords and form of a blues in C.

## Procedures

1. Have students listen to the C Blues *Band-in-a-Box* file.
2. Play the blues again for students, this time having them watch as you select the bass line to be shown in notation, using half notes for the roots of the I and V chords.

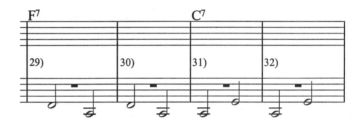

3. Show students the simplified bass line on bass xylophone or metallophone. Explain that this is an ostinato.
4. Muting the bass line, have students practice playing the ostinato (the bass line), using the half-note rhythm over the blues changes on all keyboard or barred instruments with the *Band-in-a-Box* blues file.
5. Ask students to listen to the blues again with the ostinato. Lead them in a discussion about how the ostinato is based on half notes, having them identify ways in which the part is altered to make it more interesting (rhythm changes and sometimes notes are played in different octaves).
6. Lead students in practicing the ostinato again with the blues accompaniment file, altering their ostinatos while staying with correct chord changes.
7. Ask students to play their improvised ostinatos over one chorus of the blues.

## Indicators of Success

- Students improvise ostinatos based on half notes in a jazz style over blues changes.

*(continued)*

## Follow-up

■ Have students listen to the *Band-in-a-Box* blues file used in the Procedures, but change the jazz style. Ask students to listen to and watch the notated bass line and discuss how this bass line is different from the one used in the Procedures. Have students then incorporate these ideas into their own improvised bass lines.

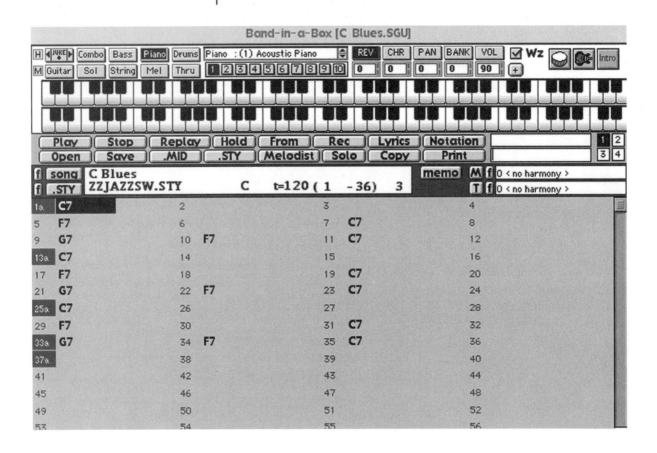

# STANDARD 3C

*Improvising melodies, variations, and accompaniments: Students improvise simple rhythmic variations and simple melodic embellishments on familiar melodies.*

## Objective

■ Students will use scat singing to improvise over a familiar song.

## Materials

■ Computer with General MIDI sound generation (internal sound card—Windows; QuickTime Musical Instruments—Macintosh) connected to powered speakers or headphones; or computer connected to General MIDI keyboard with powered speakers or headphones

■ Audiocassette recorder

■ Accompaniment software such as *Band-in-a-Box* (Victoria, BC: PG Music) or *Visual Arranger* (Buena Vista, CA: Yamaha Corporation of America)

■ Teacher-generated cassette recording of accompaniment for "The Cat Came Back," created with accompaniment software using jazz swing style

■ Song sheets for "The Cat Came Back," in g minor, generated in a notation program [*Note:* See *Share the Music*, Grade 4 (New York: Macmillan/McGraw-Hill, 1995, 2000)]

## Prior Knowledge and Experiences

■ Students have learned to sing the song "The Cat Came Back," and they understand the repetitive nature of the chord progression.

■ Students can sing chord roots on *la, sol, fa, mi* (or 6-5-4-3).

## Procedures

1. Have students sing "The Cat Came Back" with the recorded accompaniment for review and to familiarize themselves with the sound of the accompaniment.

2. Have students sing the bass line while you improvise four-bar phrases.

3. While students continue singing the bass line, improvise four-bar "questions" and pick students to give four-bar "answers" until all students have had a turn.

4. Explain to students that each question and answer (that is, each eight-bar phrase) has the space of two bass-line patterns (*la-sol-fa-mi* or 6-5-4-3) in which to scat. With students singing the bass line, repeat the song with the accompaniment and have students sing eight-bar phrases, improvising rhythmic variations and melodic embellishments on the melody of "The Cat Came Back."

## Indicators of Success

■ Students individually improvise four-bar answers to four-bar questions that fit well with the harmonic progression of "The Cat Came Back."

■ Students improvise rhythmic variations and melodic embellishments on the melody of "The Cat Came Back."

■ Students improvise variations and embellishments that fit well with the harmonic progression and that use a variety of rhythms.

## Follow-up

■ Have students improvise rhythmic variations and melodic embellishments on the melodies of other songs, such as Irving Berlin's "Blue Skies," using similar accompaniments and procedures.

# STANDARD 4A

*Composing and arranging music within specified guidelines: Students create and arrange music to accompany readings or dramatizations.*

## Objective

- Students will create and describe contrasting sections to accompany the reading of a poem.

## Materials

- Computers connected to General MIDI keyboards with powered speakers or headphones
- *Making Music* (New York: Learn Technologies Interactive) CD-ROM software
- "I Do Not Mind You Winter Wind"—poem from Jack Prelutsky's *It's Snowing, It's Snowing* (New York: Greenwillow Books, 1984), 38–39

## Prior Knowledge and Experiences

- Students have experience creating and saving music in the *Making Music* main composition space.

## Procedures

1. Read students the poem "I Do Not Mind You Winter Wind." Then ask the students to read it out loud along with you.

2. In each of the three stanzas, discuss the sound and action words, such as "whirling," "tickle me," "drifting softly," "nibble," and "bowl me over."

3. Explain to students that they will be creating a music accompaniment for the poem. Ask them to describe what music might sound like that would be a good accompaniment for each stanza. Help them use words such as "melodies moving down" for the first stanza, "soft and short sounds" for the second stanza, and "loud and thick" for the third stanza.

4. Direct students to use the *Making Music* main composition space and tools to create an accompaniment for the first stanza. Guide them in saving this music on the first "music stand."

5. Have them clear the screen and create an appropriate accompaniment for the second stanza, then save it to the second music stand. Repeat the process for the third stanza.

6. Have students combine the three accompaniments into one longer composition using the main composition space.

7. Select students to read the poem expressively while each accompaniment is played on the computer. Discuss how the elements of each composition reflect the poem.

## Indicators of Success

- Students create an accompaniment to the given poem and describe the elements of the composition using appropriate music vocabulary.

## Follow-up

- Have students create sound themes to represent the characters in a story. Play *Peter and the Wolf* by Prokofiev as an example.

*Composing and arranging music within specified guidelines:* Students create and arrange short songs and instrumental pieces within specified guidelines.

## Objective

■ Students will compose an instrumental piece that consists of a melodic ostinato, a rhythmic pattern, and a melody.

## Materials

■ Computers connected to General MIDI keyboards with powered speakers or headphones

■ Sequencing software such as *Musicshop* (Nashville: Opcode Systems) or *Master Tracks Pro* (Philadelphia: GVOX)

■ Nonpitched percussion instrument such a hand drum

■ Electronic keyboard

## Prior Knowledge and Experiences

■ Students understand the meaning of ostinato, rhythmic pattern, and melody.

■ Students have listened to examples of music that uses ostinatos (for example, "Unsquare Dance" by Dave Brubeck; Canon in D by Pachelbel; "Arabian Dance," from *The Nutcracker Suite,* by Tchaikovsky; or "O Fortuna," from *Carmina Burana,* by Orff) and have identified melodic ostinato, rhythmic pattern, and melody in one or more of these examples.

■ Students have sufficient experience with sequencing software to be able to record, copy, and paste.

## Procedures

1. Select three students to demonstrate the creation of a melodic ostinato, a rhythmic pattern, and a melody. Have one student improvise a one-measure pentatonic pattern (ostinato) on the black keys of the piano; if necessary, supply a rhythmic pattern. Ask a second student to use a nonpitched percussion instrument to improvise a one-measure rhythmic pattern that "fits" with the melodic ostinato. Have the third student improvise a melody on the electronic keyboard, using the black keys and longer note values.

2. Conduct the three students in a spontaneous arrangement by indicating to each of them either to start or stop playing at various times. Vary the texture to include each instrument in a brief solo, all three possible duet combinations, and all three instruments playing together. Discuss the performance with the class, including the order of events, the use of solos and duets to produce variety, the way the piece began, and the way the piece was brought to an end.

3. Explain that pairs of students will now work together, using the computer, keyboard, and sequencing software, to create their own compositions. Tell them they should record each part on a different track of the sequencing file. Also, explain that they should create (a) a melodic ostinato that is a one- or two-measure pattern using the black keys and a pitched instrument tone color, (b) a one-measure rhythmic pattern using a nonpitched percussion instrument, and (c) a melody with longer note values on black keys. Have them use several different textures that employ solos, duets, and trios and bring the piece to a satisfying conclusion.

4. Give students time to use the workstations, and provide feedback.

5. Ask pairs of students play their compositions for the class, and discuss successes and problems.

## Indicators of Success

■ Students create compositions that include an original melodic ostinato, a rhythmic pattern, and a melody, and that demonstrate variety, unity, and balance.

## Follow-up

■ Have students compose diatonic ostinato compositions.

*Composing and arranging music within specified guidelines: Students create and arrange short songs and instrumental pieces within specified guidelines.*

## Objective

- Students will create a short theme and two variations by altering pitch, rhythm, tempo, and tone color.

## Materials

- Computers with CD- or DVD-ROM player connected to powered speakers or headphones
- *Making Music* (New York: Learn Technologies Interactive) CD-ROM software

## Prior Knowledge and Experiences

- Students understand the concepts of pitch and duration.

## Procedures

1. Using the "Melody and Rhythm Maker" section of *Making Music,* demonstrate how to place bird icons (pitches) on the telephone wires (scale steps) to create a pitch row. Demonstrate how to create a rhythmic pattern by clicking on eggs in the egg row to "hatch" them (make them sound). (Each egg represents a beat. A hatched egg will sound a note; an unhatched egg represents a rest.) Then demonstrate how to create notes of longer duration by clicking on an egg and dragging the cursor to the right.

2. By pressing the corresponding green arrows, play the pitch and rhythm rows back and demonstrate several revisions of each row.

3. With students working alone or in pairs, ask them to create a pitch and rhythm row using the same techniques that you have demonstrated. Encourage them to listen carefully to each row and to make revisions as they work.

4. Once the students have completed their rows, demonstrate how to combine them into the graphic composition space by pressing the blue arrow. Demonstrate the process of listening to the resulting melody and separating the pitches and rhythms in order to make revisions.

5. Ask students to use the instrument palette to select different instrument tone colors for their melodies. Encourage them to experiment with the tempo of the melody by adjusting the slider bar.

6. Ask students to select the best instrument and tempo for their melodies. When students are satisfied with their melodies, have them save their work to one of the "music stands" below the composition space.

7. Ask students to make two variations of their melodies (themes) by combining the same pitch row with a different rhythm row. Have them save each variation on a separate music stand. Ask students to play their themes for the class and to talk about their compositional decisions. Encourage the class to offer constructive suggestions.

## Indicators of Success

- Students create a melody and two variations.

- Students describe their compositional decisions.

## Follow-up

- Have students use the themes they created in the Procedures to form a larger theme-and-variation composition in the composition space using the copy tool, retrograde, inversion, and dynamics. Have them experiment with different scales using the "stair steps" to create variations using the minor and pentatonic scales. Encourage them to add a harmonizing part to each of their melodies.

# STANDARD 4C

*Composing and arranging music within specified guidelines:* Students use a variety of sound sources when composing.

## Objective

- Students will create a free-form sound story using a variety of tone colors and music elements and describe the composition using appropriate music vocabulary.

## Materials

- Electronic keyboards with built-in speakers
- Headphones

## Prior Knowledge and Experiences

- Students understand the concepts of high and low notes, short and long durations, soft and loud sounds, different tone colors of instruments, thick and thin textures, and other basic music elements.
- Students are familiar with the various tone color or timbre possibilities and accompaniment features of the electronic keyboard.

## Procedures

1. Explain that students will be using the electronic keyboards to create a sound story suggesting a mood, an activity, or an animal. To prepare students for listening closely to the tone color, or special quality, of sounds, ask them to close their eyes and listen closely to the sounds of the room (fans blowing, people breathing, machines running). Have students name these sounds and try to describe them using words such as "soft," "low," "scratchy," "repeating," and "rattling."

2. Repeat the process with sounds heard outside and sounds that might be heard in places such as the mall or the doctor's office, in the city or the country, or at home.

3. Have students listen to several different tone color or timbre possibilities on the electronic keyboards, such as "orchestra bells" or "saw wave," and use words to describe the tone color of each tone color selection (for example, "bright," "dark," "edgy," "harsh," "smooth," or "rough"). With a time limit of five minutes, have students select one tone color and improvise a short piece to suggest a mood or a simple story.

4. Have students listen to and discuss some of the improvisations, helping students use appropriate vocabulary (such as "high," "low," "soft," "loud," "thick," "thin," "short," "long") to describe tone color and music elements. Discuss what makes some compositions more interesting than others.

5. Discuss subject ideas for sound stories—for example: moods such as happy, sad, excited, or surprised; activities such as skating, snow sledding, climbing, or bike riding; and animals such as rabbits, horses, lions, elephants, dinosaurs, or birds.

6. Give students time to create three more short mood or sound story pieces. Specify guidelines such as using high and low notes, thick and thin textures, a variety of tone colors, black keys only or black-and-white key combinations, or vocal sounds or singing. Ask students to give titles to their compositions.

7. Have students perform their compositions, describe their stories, and explain how they used the elements of music. Discuss what makes some compositions more interesting than others.

## Indicators of Success

- Students create sound stories using a variety of tone colors and music elements.

- Students explain their compositions using appropriate music vocabulary and descriptive words.

## Follow-up

- Have students record their compositions using a tape recorder, the built-in recorder in the keyboard, or sequencing software on a computer. Give them the opportunity to present their compositions to others in the classroom or in an activity for parents.

# STANDARD 5A

*Reading and notating music: Students read whole, half, dotted half, quarter, and eighth notes and rests in 2/4, 3/4, and 4/4 meter signatures.*

## Objective

■ Students will read and write four-beat rhythmic patterns using quarter and eighth notes and quarter rests.

## Materials

■ Computers with CD- or DVD-ROM player connected to powered speakers or headphones

■ *Music Ace 2* (Chicago: Harmonic Vision) CD-ROM software

■ Teacher-prepared progress worksheet (see page 25) for students to keep a record of their progress and scores

■ Teacher-prepared rhythm test (see Rhythm Test) with several test items showing two different four-beat rhythmic patterns (for each item, the student must identify which of the two patterns the teacher is playing); and a few items in which students must write down four-beat rhythmic patterns that they hear played

■ Copies of handout with several four-beat rhythmic patterns (see step 1); or notation on the board

## Prior Knowledge and Experiences

■ Students have experience echoing basic four-beat rhythms.

■ Students can identify quarter and eighth notes and quarter rest, and they have experience using them to notate simple four-beat patterns that they hear.

## Procedures

1. To prepare students to use the rhythm lessons and games in *Music Ace 2,* echo clap and count several four-beat patterns that use quarter and eighth notes and quarter rests. Help them read and play a few four-beat patterns written on a handout or the board.

2. Distribute the worksheet for tracking progress. Have students open *Music Ace 2* and move to Session 5, "Basic Rhythm Notation." Have them work through the lessons, then the games, in which students identify rhythms they hear as same or different, echo-play rhythms that they hear, play rhythms that they see in notation, and write down rhythms that they hear. Ask them to check off each lesson and game on the worksheet when they finish it. You may also want to set a minimum acceptable score for students to achieve for the games before moving ahead.

3. Have students move to Session 6, "The Quarter Rest." Repeat the procedure from step 2.

4. When students have completed the lessons and games, give them the listening and writing test (see Rhythm Test).

## Indicators of Success

■ Students identify correct notation for four-beat rhythmic patterns that they hear.

■ Students write correct rhythm notation for four-beat patterns that they hear.

## Follow-up

■ Have students notate several of their own four-beat patterns. Then have students practice playing the patterns or have another student play them.

■ Have students identify four-beat patterns in songs and then count and clap the patterns as the songs are being sung.

# Progress Worksheet
## Music Ace 2
### Sessions 5 and 6

Name _____

Check off each lesson and game after you complete it.

| Session 5: Basic Rhythm Notation | | Session 6: The Quarter Rest | |
|---|---|---|---|
| **Lesson** | **Game** | **Lesson** | **Game** |
| 1. | 1. | 1. | 1. |
| 2. | 2. | 2. | 2. |
| 3. | 3. | 3. | 3. |
| 4. | 4. | 4. | 4. |
| | 5. | | 5. |

# Rhythm Test

Name:_____

**Circle the rhythm you hear.**

**Write the rhythm you hear.**

| | | | |
|---|---|---|---|
| **1** | ♩ ♩ ♫ ♩ | ♫ ♩ ♩ ♩ | **6** _____ |
| **2** | ♩ ♫ ♫ ♩ | ♫ ♩ ♫ ♩ | **7** _____ |
| **3** | ♩ ♩ ♫ ♫ | ♫ ♫ ♩ ♩ | **8** _____ |
| **4** | ♩ 𝄽 ♫ ♩ | ♫ ♩ 𝄽 ♩ | **9** _____ |
| **5** | ♫ 𝄽 ♫ | ♫ ♩ ♩ 𝄽 | **10** _____ |

*Reading and notating music: Students use a system (syllables, numbers, or letters) to read simple pitch notation in the treble clef in major keys.*

## Objective

- Students will sing and play original simple melodies on keyboard.

## Materials

- Computers connected to MIDI keyboards and powered speakers or headphones and printer

- Notation software such as *Music Time* (Philadelphia: GVOX), *Encore* (Philadelphia: GVOX), or *Print Music* (Eden Prairie, MN: Coda Music Technology)

## Prior Knowledge and Experiences

- Students can read and sing music using solfège syllables.

- Students have written melodic patterns or short melodies.

- Students have performed written melodies on barred instruments or keyboards.

## Procedures

1. Review with students the reading of common solfège syllable patterns from music notation in treble clef, beginning with *do, re, mi,* and *sol.*

2. Help students transfer the solfège patterns to appropriate keys on the keyboard.

3. Have students use notation software to enter (by clicking in notes) two or three melodic patterns with four to eight notes, using the notes for the solfège syllables they just practiced (for example: *do, re, mi, sol*). Ask them to try to sing the patterns they entered, then listen to the patterns as played back by the notation software to check if they sang correctly. Also, have them try to perform these patterns on the keyboard and again listen to the patterns, using the notation software to compare what they play with what they hear.

4. Have each student notate an original eight-measure melody in 3/4 or 4/4 meter. After they have entered their melodies, ask students to sing their melodies and to play them on the keyboard. Have them listen to their melodies as played back by the notation software and compare what they are singing and playing to the correct version played by the software, repeating until they have corrected their errors.

5. As a final check on their ability to play their melodies, have students record their melodies into the notation software as they play them on the keyboard in real time. Have students compare their recorded versions with the versions they entered by clicking in notes.

6. Have students demonstrate their melodies for the class by playing on the keyboard and by listening to the melodies played back by the notation software. Print students' melodies for them to practice again later.

## Indicators of Success

- Students accurately sing and play on the keyboard original melodic patterns and simple melodies based on familiar solfège patterns.

## Follow-up

- As students grow in their ability to sing written solfège patterns, repeat the activities in the Procedures with additional notes.

- Give students prepared notated melodies in notation software files and have them play these on keyboards, comparing their performance to the melodies as played back by the notation software.

# STANDARD 5D

***Reading and notating music:** Students use standard symbols to notate meter, rhythm, pitch, and dynamics in simple patterns presented by the teacher.*

## Objective

- Students will notate pitches for a poem set to music and create an original ending for the song.

## Materials

- Computers with General MIDI sound generation (internal sound card—Windows; QuickTime Musical Instruments—Macintosh) connected to powered speakers or headphones; or computers connected to General MIDI keyboards with powered speakers or headphones

- Notation software such as *Music Time* (Philadelphia: GVOX) or *Print Music* (Eden Prairie, MN: Coda Music Technology), configured to play sound using the internal General MIDI sound source; or software configured to play sound using the General MIDI keyboard

- Copies of words and rhythms for the first verse of the poem "Skyscraper"; or for another four-line children's poem

## Prior Knowledge and Experiences

- Students can place notes on the staff using notation software.

- Students are able to notate simple melodic patterns that they hear sung or played.

## Procedures

1. Help students learn to sing the first two lines of the poem "Skyscraper" (below) with a melody you create based on the notes *do, re, mi*. Give students copies of the poem's first verse with the rhythms under the words.

Copyright 1974 by Dennis Lee. From *Alligator Pie* by Dennis Lee and Frank Newfeld (Toronto: Macmillan, 1974). Reprinted with permission.

2. Using notation software, review with students how to click in notes on the correct lines and spaces for *do, re, mi* in a key you choose (such as F or G). Also, review how to click two eighth notes together to create a beamed pair of eighth notes.

3. Have students sing each line of "Skyscraper" to themselves and then try to notate the correct pitches for the melody, using the rhythms on their printed copies of the poem. Remind them to listen for whether the melody is moving up or down and whether the notes are stepping or skipping.

4. Give students time to work and help them correct errors until they have successfully notated the pitches and rhythms for the first two lines. Encourage them to listen carefully to what they are notating and to compare what they hear to the correct way to sing the song.

5. After they have finished the first two lines, encourage students to choose their own notes (using *do, re, mi*) for the last two lines of the song and then try to sing it.

6. Have students take turns singing their song endings after the class sings the first and second lines of the song as it is played back by the notation software.

## Indicators of Success

- Students notate pitches and rhythms for the first two lines of "Skyscraper."

- Students create an original melody for the last two lines of the poem's first verse.

- Students accurately sing the melody for the song.

## Follow-up

- Repeat the Procedures with other poems using more pitches.

- Have students create both rhythms and pitches for a melody based on a poem.

# STANDARD 6B

*Listening to, analyzing, and describing music: Students demonstrate perceptual skills by moving, by answering questions about, and by describing aural examples of music of various styles representing diverse cultures.*

## Objective

- Students will identify same, similar, and different phrases aurally and visually.

## Materials

- Computers with General MIDI sound generation (internal sound card—Windows; QuickTime Musical Instruments—Macintosh) connected to powered speakers or headphones; or computers connected to General MIDI keyboards with powered speakers or headphones

- Notation software such as *Music Time* (Philadelphia: GVOX) or *Print Music* (Eden Prairie, MN: Coda Music Technology)

- Teacher-prepared *Music Time* files for "Deck the Halls" and several other songs that clearly show same/different phrase structure

## Prior Knowledge and Experiences

- Students have experience analyzing phrases.

- Students have sung songs with same/similar and contrasting phrases.

- Students have used movement to show beginning and ending of phrases.

## Procedures

1. Review the concept of a phrase. Help students identify same/similar and different phrases in a familiar song.

2. Instruct students to listen to the first example from the files you have prepared.

3. Instruct students to locate the color palette and use the cursor in the pointer mode to highlight phrases and change their color. Have them change phrases that are the same to the same color and use different colors to mark phrases that are different.

4. Have students check their work by listening to the musical selection again and making any necessary changes.

5. Repeat steps 2–4 using other songs in the files you have prepared.

6. Ask students to save their work for teacher assessment.

## Indicators of Success

- Students identify phrases that are the same or different by using notation software to mark similar and different phrases.

## Follow-up

- Have students identify same and different phrases in a similar manner using more complex music examples.

*Listening to, analyzing, and describing music:* Students identify the sounds of a variety of instruments, including many orchestra and band instruments, and instruments from various cultures, as well as children's voices and male and female adult voices.

## Objective

■ Students will describe and identify percussion instruments heard in MIDI songs and classify them into groups of instruments that are hit, scraped, and shaken.

## Materials

■ Computer with General MIDI sound generation (internal sound card—Windows; QuickTime Musical Instruments—Macintosh) connected to powered speakers or headphones; or computer connected to General MIDI keyboards with powered speakers or headphones

■ Computer display projector and screen

■ *Band-in-a-Box* accompaniment software (Victoria, BC: PG Music)

■ *Band-in-a-Box* manual, "Drum Window" chapter (includes pictures of percussion instruments and QWERTY keys that play instruments)

## Prior Knowledge and Experiences

■ Students have experience playing a variety of percussion instruments and recognize that some are hit, some are scraped, and some are shaken.

■ Students can identify the percussion instruments they have played in their classroom.

## Procedures

1. Have students review correct methods for playing classroom percussion instruments. Ask them to classify the instruments into groups that are played by hitting, scraping, and shaking. Also have them identify which of the instruments are drums.

2. Play the "Mambo" demonstration song file located in the *Band-in-a-Box* folder. Have students watch on the computer screen the instruments being played as the song plays.

3. Have students identify percussion instruments in the "Drum Window" chapter that they think played in the song "Mambo."

4. Run the mouse over the instruments in the "Drum Window" in the *Band-in-a-Box* manual, and have students read the name of each percussion instrument to see if they have correctly identified the instruments. Then click on each instrument so that the students can hear the instruments.

5. Have students identify whether each instrument is hit, scraped, or shaken.

6. Repeat the steps above for demonstrations of the following: "Bossa," "Cha Cha," "Mexican," "Reggae 2" or "Reggae 3," and "Rhumba." Have students compare which styles use the most percussion instruments that are hit, the most that are scraped, and the most that are shaken.

## Indicators of Success

■ Students identify percussion instruments played in the *Band-in-a-Box* program by sight and by sound.

■ Students classify percussion instruments into groups of instruments that are hit, scraped, or shaken.

## Follow-up

■ Prepare a *Band-in-a-Box* MIDI file based on a song students have learned in class. Have students record themselves first playing *Band-in-a-Box* instruments with the song and then playing classroom instruments. Ask them to compare the two versions.

*Listening to, analyzing, and describing music: Students identify the sounds of a variety of instruments, including many orchestra and band instruments, and instruments from various cultures, as well as children's voices and male and female adult voices.*

## Objective

- Students will identify a variety of instruments and voices heard in African music.

## Materials

- Computers with CD- or DVD-ROM player connected to powered speakers or head-phones
- *Rock Rap 'n Roll* (Reading, MA: Scott Foresman) software, with teacher's guide
- Copies for students of "Careful Listening" worksheet (page 19 in *Rock Rap 'n Roll* teacher's guide)

## Prior Knowledge and Experiences

- Students have experience listening to a variety of instruments and can identify percussion, brass, and woodwind instruments.
- Students can identify male and female adult singing voices.
- Students have studied and listened to African music.

## Procedures

1. Have students work in pairs on workstations, listening to Song Loops in the Africa section of the *Rock Rap 'n Roll* software.
2. Ask students to identify on the "Careful Listening" worksheet the instruments they hear in each loop.
3. Have students listen to Voc-A-Lizer sounds on the *Rock Rap 'n Roll* software and identify on the worksheet which samples are sung and which are spoken.
4. Ask students to play the QWERTY keys on the computer keyboard and identify on the worksheet whether each sound is a percussion, brass, woodwind, or voice sound.
5. Discuss with students instruments they heard in the Africa section of the *Rock Rap 'n Roll* software. Where possible, show and play real instruments to reinforce learning.
6. Discuss with students the voices they heard in the Africa section of the program. [*Note:* Students will hear mostly male adult voices; they may be able to hear women's voices singing with male voices in some of the Song Loops, but there are no children's voices.]
7. Have students describe where in the program they heard spoken voice sounds and singing voice sounds.

## Indicators of Success

- Students identify percussion, woodwind, and brass instruments in short African musical examples.
- Students identify male and female adult voices in short African musical examples and distinguish when the voice is speaking or singing.

## Follow-up

- Have students arrange the Song Loops into a sequence and improvise with the new sequence of sounds using QWERTY keys and mouse. Then have them record a final copy and discuss how they use sounds to create a song with the background Song Loops.

# STANDARD 7A

*Evaluating music and music performances:* Students devise criteria for evaluating performances and compositions.

## Objective

- Students will devise criteria for evaluating their compositions and use the criteria to offer suggestions for improvement.

## Materials

- Computers with CD-ROM drives connected to powered speakers or headphones
- *Making Music* (New York: Learn Technologies Interactive) CD-ROM software

## Prior Knowledge and Experiences

- Students have successfully completed compositions, using *Making Music* software, illustrating use of a music element (such as thick texture or soft dynamics, or illustrating calmness, energy, light-heartedness, or another expressive quality).
- Students can use appropriate terminology for describing the element being studied (for example: thick or thin texture, bright or dark tone color) or for describing how an expressive quality was conveyed by music elements.
- Students have listened to and described compositions that clearly use an element being studied (for example, texture, or dynamics) or that convey an expressive quality.

## Procedures

1. Brainstorm with the class about how they might decide whether a composition did a good job of illustrating an element or quality.
2. After brainstorming, help the class decide on terms to describe these characteristics. For example, for compositions that illustrate the use of an energetic quality, the criteria might be: (a) uses many short notes, (b) uses louder dynamics, and (c) uses fast upward and downward melodies.
3. Write the criteria on the board along with a 1–5 rating scale, or make a worksheet to hand out to students.
4. Have the class listen to the selected compositions they created previously using *Making Music* software. After listening, help them use the criteria they have devised to rate the compositions.
5. Ask students to make positive suggestions for changing the compositions to better meet the criteria.

## Indicators of Success

- Students devise criteria for evaluating their compositions.
- Students use the criteria to offer suggestions for improving their compositions.

## Follow-up

- Give students time to change their compositions by applying the suggestions for improvement that classmates offered. Ask students to explain what changes they made to better illustrate the use of various elements.
- Have students repeat the Procedures, focusing on another music element (such as long and short durations) or two elements at the same time (such as dynamics and tempo).

# STANDARD 8A

*Understanding relationships between music, the other arts, and disciplines outside the arts: Students identify similarities and differences in the meanings of common terms used in the various arts.*

## Objective

- Students will identify repeated and contrasting sections in music and describe how elements of visual art and music create ABA form in given examples.

## Materials

- Computer that has Internet access and General MIDI sound generation (internal sound card—Windows; QuickTime Musical Instruments—Macintosh) connected to powered speakers or headphones
- Computer display projector and screen
- Web browser software such as *Netscape Communicator* (Mountain View, CA: Netscape) or *Internet Explorer* (Redmond, WA: Microsoft Corporation), with bookmarks to a children's music site such as KIDiddles (http://www.kididdles.com); and a classical music site such as Classical Archives (http://www.prs.net)
- National Gallery of Art web site (http://www.nga.gov); or another art site

## Prior Knowledge and Experiences

- Students can identify the basic elements (such as shape and color) of visual art.
- Students can identify repeated sections in music.

## Procedures

1. Use the computer and projector to display the lyrics and play back "Twinkle, Twinkle, Little Star" or another short song in ABA form from the KIDiddles web site. Lead students in singing the song. Discuss the structure of the song, pointing out that the first section is repeated and that the middle section differs.

2. Go to the Classical Archives site and play the A section of "Dance of the Sugar Plum Fairy" or of another example in ABA form. Guide students in creating an appropriate dance movement for the A section.

3. Play the entire "Dance of the Sugar Plum Fairy" after instructing students to move during the A sections and "freeze" during the B section.

4. To lead students to recognize ABA form, ask them (a) how many times in the composition they began moving, (b) when in the composition the movement started, and (c) what happened in the composition between episodes of movement.

5. From the National Gallery site, display several pieces of art that suggest ABA form (for example, "Reflections" by William Merrit Chase or "Spring Garden" by Crispijn van de Passe). Have students describe the repeated and contrasting visual elements that create ABA form in each example.

## Indicators of Success

- Students move during repeated sections of music and freeze during the contrasting section of music in ABA form.
- Students identify and describe repeated and contrasting elements in visual art.

## Follow-up

- Have students use crayons or paint to create a piece of visual art in ABA form. Ask students to show their work to the class and explain their use of ABA form. Then review with the class how ABA form is used in a similar manner in music.

# STANDARD 8B

*Understanding relationships between music, the other arts, and disciplines outside the arts:* Students identify ways in which the principles and subject matter of other disciplines taught in the school are interrelated with those of music.

## Objective

- Students will compose introductory and background music, write an accompanying story, and dramatize the story.

## Materials

- General MIDI keyboards
- Audiocassette recorder with microphone and blank tape
- Videocassette recorder and blank tape
- Video monitor

## Prior Knowledge and Experiences

- Students have some experience composing and improvising.

## Procedures

1. Divide class into groups and have groups of students collaborate to compose introductory music for a play on keyboards. You may wish to instruct students to use only the black keys in their compositions.

2. Assist groups in performing and recording their work to audiotape.

3. Instruct groups to determine the mood of their compositions and write a story to go along with the mood of the music.

4. Encourage groups to create background music, sound effects, and so forth to accompany their stories. Record each composition as groups complete their compositions.

5. Have students rehearse dramatizing their stories, playing cassettes at the appropriate times as background music. Use the videocamera to record each scene after it is rehearsed.

6. Show the videotapes to the class and discuss how the music reinforces the mood of the stories. In the discussion, have students answer the following questions: How did the accompanying music illustrate the story? How well did the background music and sound effects represent the characters and events in the story? What did the actors do to make the story convincing? Videotape the discussion.

## Indicators of Success

- Students compose introductory and background music and write an accompanying story.
- Students dramatize their stories and describe how the music illustrates the story and represents the characters and events.

## Follow-up

- Have students create costumes and build sets for the stories they created in the Procedures. Videotape the new versions of the dramatizations to play back at a parents' meeting.

# STANDARD 9B

*Understanding music in relation to history and culture:* Students describe in simple terms how elements of music are used in music examples from various cultures of the world.

## Objective

- Students will create multi-layered complex rhythms based on West African musical styles and describe the use of texture and rhythm in their compositions.

## Materials

- Computers with CD- or DVD-ROM player connected to powered speakers or headphones
- *Making More Music* (New York: Learn Technologies Interactive) software
- Sound files of West African percussion groups, downloaded from the Internet—for example, Ancient Future (http://www.ancient-future.com) or RootsWorld (http://www.rootsworld.com)

## Prior Knowledge and Experiences

- Students have sung, played, and moved in 3/4 meter and 4/4 meter.

## Procedures

1. Review with students how music is organized into meter groupings of 2, 3, 4, and so on.
2. Play downloaded files of West African percussion groups, and explain how each instrument may be playing in a different meter.
3. Demonstrate to students how to use *Making More Music's* "Rhythm Band" option to "paint" rhythmic patterns.
4. Have students create eight-measure rhythmic patterns for five different instruments, varying the meter from one instrument to another, as in the West African percussion music they heard. Tell them to click on the "composition book" and save the file with their name when they are finished.
5. Have students present their compositions to the class and discuss whether their compositions are in a single meter or in multi-meters. Discuss with them how their use of texture and rhythm makes their compositions in the style of West African percussion music.

## Indicators of Success

- Students create multi-layered rhythm compositions.
- Students identify the meters used by the various instruments in their compositions.
- Students describe the use of the elements of texture and rhythm in music based on West African musical styles.

## Follow-up

- Teach students to perform a multi-layered rhythm based on West African styles.

# GENERAL MUSIC
## Grades 5-8

***Singing, alone and with others, a varied repertoire of music:*** *Students sing accurately and with good breath control throughout their singing ranges, alone and in small and large ensembles.*

## Objective

- Students will accurately sing with good breath control in small ensembles and record their favorite songs for young children.

## Materials

- Computers that have microphones, connected to powered speakers or headphones
- Multimedia software such as *HyperStudio* (Torrance, CA: Knowledge Adventure), *PowerPoint* (Redmond, WA: Microsoft Corporation), or *AppleWorks* (Cupertino, CA: Apple Computer)

## Prior Knowledge and Experiences

- Students have experience using computer drawing, painting, and text tools.

## Procedures

1. Divide the class into small groups and have each group prepare text and graphics for one screen of a slide show. Explain that each screen should contain the lyrics for the group's favorite song for small children.

2. Ask each group to create a button and record the group's singing of a selected song accurately and with good breath control. Explain that when the button is clicked, the recording should play.

3. After all songs are entered, prepare a slide containing an index of songs with hypertext links to the appropriate slides.

4. Help students design and create a title-page slide.

5. Have students play and view the entire slide show.

## Indicators of Success

- Students sing accurately and with good breath control.
- Students record their performances.
- Students play their slide show and recordings for the class.

## Follow-up

- Arrange for students to demonstrate the slide show for a first- or second-grade class. On specified days, have small groups of students use their slide to teach first- or second-graders their selected song.

*Singing, alone and with others, a varied repertoire of music: Students sing accurately and with good breath control throughout their singing ranges, alone and in small and large ensembles.*

## Objective

- Students will sing, accurately and with good breath control, melodies they have composed with their own MIDI accompaniments.

## Materials

- Computers that have Internet access and microphones, connected to General MIDI keyboards with powered speakers or headphones
- Printer for computers
- Sequencing software with digital audio such as *Cakewalk Home Studio* (Cambridge, MA: Cakewalk), *Metro 5* (Cambridge, MA: Cakewalk), or *MicroLogic AV* (Grass Valley, CA: Emagic Soft- und Hardware GmbH/Emagic, Inc.)
- Audiocassette recorder, microphone, and blank tape

## Prior Knowledge and Experiences

- Students have experience with sequencing operations.
- Students have experience composing melodies and accompaniments.

## Procedures

1. Divide the class into small groups, and help each group of students brainstorm to write a short radio play with episodes in which individual characters sing to develop the plot.
2. Have each student select an episode and compose a song with MIDI accompaniment that develops the plot of the story.
3. Ask each group to practice singing its song. Emphasize the need for singing accurately and with good breath control.
4. Help groups record their plays (including narration, dialogue, sound effects, and singing) to audiotape. Remind students again to sing accurately and with good breath control.

## Indicators of Success

- Students compose melodies with MIDI accompaniments for individual characters in radio plays they have created.
- Students sing their melodies accurately and with good breath control.

## Follow-up

- Help students post their recordings as audio files to the school's web site.
- Ask for volunteer groups of students to perform their plays with live singing for a school assembly.

# STANDARD 1C

*Singing, alone and with others, a varied repertoire of music:* Students sing music representing diverse genres and cultures, with expression appropriate for the work being performed.

## Objective

- Students will sing rock-and-roll tunes with appropriate expression.

## Materials

- Computers that have Internet access and microphones, connected to General MIDI keyboards with powered speakers or headphones

- Sequencing software with digital audio such as *Cakewalk Home Studio* (Cambridge, MA: Cakewalk), *Metro 5* (Cambridge, MA: Cakewalk), or *MicroLogic AV* (Grass Valley, CA: Emagic Soft- und Hardware GmbH/Emagic, Inc.)

## Prior Knowledge and Experiences

- Students have experience searching Internet sites, printing web pages, and downloading files.

## Procedures

1. Divide the class into small groups of students, and ask each group to search the Internet for a 1960's rock-and-roll tune with lyrics and chord symbols that they can download and print.

2. Have each group download a MIDI file of its selected tune and print the lyrics and chord symbols. Ask the groups to write their names and the name of the MIDI file on their printouts.

3. Show students how to import their MIDI files into the sequencing program. Then, have them learn to sing the selected songs expressively by following the printed lyrics and playing back the sequence.

4. When students have learned their songs, have them record their vocal performances on an audio track of the sequence and save their files. Emphasize the importance of expressive singing.

5. Play back the sequences for the class, and discuss each group's success in singing its song with appropriate expression for the rock-and-roll style.

## Indicators of Success

- Students demonstrate appropriate vocal expression in their performances of rock-and-roll tunes.

## Follow-up

- Prepare a *Band-in-a-Box* (Victoria, BC: PG Music) rock-and-roll accompaniment for a medley of the tunes. Have the entire class perform the medley with appropriate expression.

# STANDARD 3A

*Improvising melodies, variations, and accompaniments: Students improvise simple harmonic accompaniments.*

## Objective

- Students will improvise a harmonic accompaniment for a blues melody.

## Materials

- Computers connected to General MIDI keyboards with powered speakers or headphones
- Sequencing software such as *Musicshop* (Nashville: Opcode Systems) or *Cakewalk Home Studio* (Cambridge, MA: Cakewalk)
- *Dick Hyman's Century of Jazz Piano* CD-ROM (West New York, NJ: JSS Music, 1998)
- Transcriptions of selected solos on Hyman CD-ROM (optional)
- Teacher-generated blues melodies, in the key of C, saved as separate MIDI files in the sequencing program

## Prior Knowledge and Experiences

- Students know how to use the workstation hardware and sequencing software.
- Students understand the basic chord progression of the blues.
- Students have listened to various pianists (such as Mary Lou Williams, Duke Ellington, and Oscar Peterson) playing the blues and have discussed accompaniment styles.

## Procedures

1. Have students practice playing bass lines, using roots and fifths of the I, IV, and V7 chords.

2. Using *Dick Hyman's Century of Jazz Piano* CD-ROM, direct students to listen for how Williams, Ellington, and Peterson accompany the blues on piano (that is, what the pianist does with the bass line in the left hand and with chords in the right hand). Have them note, for example, Williams's boogie-woogie style, Ellington's stride piano style, and Peterson's contemporary sound.

3. Distribute transcriptions of the solos on the CD-ROM, and guide students in a discussion of how the harmonic accompaniment differs in blues recordings by each pianist.

4. Have each student select one of the melodies on the sequencing program and experiment at the keyboard with improvising a harmonic accompaniment for the melody. Ask students to select a piano, guitar, organ, or vibraphone sound to create chordal accompaniments using at least two notes of the chord.

5. Have students continue to improvise their accompaniments with the recorded MIDI melodies.

6. Ask students to record their improvised accompaniments.

## Indicators of Success

- Students improvise harmonic accompaniments for given blues melodies.

## Follow-up

- Play back the student improvisations created in the Procedures. Have students record percussion parts and improvised solos to complete their blues arrangements.

# STANDARD 3B

*Improvising melodies, variations, and accompaniments: Students improvise melodic embellishments and simple rhythmic and melodic variations on given pentatonic melodies and melodies in major keys.*

## Objective

- Students will create an arrangement of a given song by improvising melodic embellishments and rhythmic variations.

## Materials

- Computers with CD- or DVD-ROM player connected to powered speakers or headphones
- *Rock Rap 'n Roll* (Reading, MA: Scott Foresman) software and accompanying teacher's guide
- Copies for students of "Careful Listening" worksheet, from *Rock Rap 'n Roll* teacher's guide, in a style that students have selected (for example, African or Latin)
- Copies of blank screen *Rock Rap 'n Roll* template, from the inside back cover of the *Rock Rap 'n Roll* teacher's guide

## Prior Knowledge and Experiences

- Students have some experience creating arrangements in various styles in the *Rock Rap 'n Roll* software by "dragging" sequences.
- Students have experience recording and saving files with the *Rock Rap 'n Roll* software.

## Procedures

1. Have students listen to the Song Loops (short sequences that can be arranged in any order to create songs) in the selected style in the *Rock Rap 'n Roll* software. Distribute the "Careful Listening" worksheet for the selected style, and have students complete the worksheet.

2. Distribute blank screen *Rock Rap 'n Roll* template and instruct students to sketch out their plans for their improvisations on the template and experiment with and practice their arrangements.

3. Guide students to write on the template when they will use the Vibe-A-Tron, Bop-O-Rama, Voc-A-Lizer, Key Map, and Pitch 'Em for melodic embellishments and rhythmic variations. Explain to students that they will (a) use pitched sounds correlated with QWERTY row of keys on computer keyboard to improvise melodic embellishments on their arrangements, and (b) identify and use nonpitched percussion sounds to improvise rhythmic variations on their arrangements.

4. Instruct students to record their improvisations. Then have them improvise melodic embellishments and rhythmic variations with chosen Vibe-A-Tron, Bop-O-Rama, Voc-A-Lizer, Key Map, and Pitch 'Em while their arrangements are played back.

5. Have each student select his or her favorite arrangement for assessment.

## Indicators of Success

- Students improvise melodic embellishments and rhythmic variations in the selected style.

## Follow-up

- Have students play back for the class the arrangements they created in the Procedures. Lead the class in a discussion of the effectiveness of each improvisation, including how it meets the parameters given to the students for their improvisations.
- Repeat the Procedures using another style on the *Rock Rap 'n Roll* software.

*Improvising melodies, variations, and accompaniments: Students improvise short melodies, unaccompanied and over given rhythmic accompaniments, each in a consistent style, meter, and tonality.*

## Objective

- Students will improvise an eight-bar melody over a half-note or dotted-rhythm accompaniment in a given style.

## Materials

- Computers connected to General MIDI keyboards with powered speakers or headphones

- Sequencing software such as *Musicshop* (Nashville: Opcode Systems) or *Cakewalk Home Studio* (Cambridge, MA: Cakewalk)

- Teacher-generated eight-bar accompaniments (one using half notes and the other using dotted rhythms) in different styles (such as bossa nova, rock, swing, and blues) in sequencing program

## Prior Knowledge and Experiences

- Students have some experience using the selected sequencing software.

- Students understand note limitations of using fourteen white keys for their improvisations. [*Note:* Mark this fourteen-note range of keys with masking tape.]

## Procedures

1. Demonstrate improvising of a melody with two of the given accompaniments (one with half notes and the other with dotted rhythms). Discuss with students how to create melodic improvisations that complement the style, meter, and tonality of a selected accompaniment.

2. Have students choose the style and the accompaniment (half notes or dotted rhythms) they would like to use for their improvisations. Then have them select an instrument from the General MIDI sound bank for both the melodic improvisation and the accompaniment part.

3. Guide students in improvising melodies (within the marked fourteen-white-key range) with their selected accompaniments. Have students record and save their improvisations.

4. Have students create and record several different improvisations for the selected accompaniment. Ask each student to select his or her best improvisation for assessment. Remind them that the melodic improvisation should complement the style, meter, and tonality of the selected accompaniment.

## Indicators of Success

- Students improvise melodies within the fourteen-white-key range.

- Students improvise melodies that complement the accompaniment in style, meter, and tonality.

## Follow-up

- Have students play for the class the melodic improvisations they created in the Procedures. Guide students in discussing how well each improvisation complements the style, meter, and tonality of the selected accompaniment.

- Repeat the Procedures, having students improvise melodies over accompaniments in another style.

*Improvising melodies, variations, and accompaniments:* Students improvise short melodies, unaccompanied and over given rhythmic accompaniments, each in a consistent style, meter, and tonality.

## Objective

■ Students will improvise pentatonic melodies over two different accompaniment patterns of differing styles.

## Materials

■ Computers connected to General MIDI keyboards with powered speakers or headphones

■ Accompaniment software such as *Band-in-a-Box* (Victoria, BC: PG Music) or *Visual Arranger* (Buena Vista, CA: Yamaha Corporation of America)

■ Teacher-prepared templates in accompaniment software with chords (eight bars as listed below) to harmonize with the pentatonic scale beginning on B-flat (B-flat, C, E-flat, F, G)

1. E-flat  2. cm  3. A-flat
4. E-flat 5. E-flat  6. cm
7. A-flat  8. E-flat

## Prior Knowledge and Experiences

■ Students can name the notes in the pentatonic scale beginning on B-flat.

■ Students have listened to computer-generated improvised solos and have discussed what makes each solo complement the given accompaniment style.

## Procedures

1. Review with students the notes in the pentatonic scale beginning on B-flat.

2. Using external speakers for the accompaniment file you created, demonstrate for the class an eight-bar improvised solo using the B-flat pentatonic scale over the accompaniment file.

3. Lead a discussion about how you improvised a solo using the five notes from the pentatonic scale. Explain how to think about improvising in a style, noting that if the accompaniment is in swing style, for example, the improvised melody needs to be in the same style.

4. Have students practice improvising eight-bar improvised solos using the B-flat pentatonic scale with accompaniment.

5. Have students change the style in *Band-in-a-Box* and improvise solos in the new style.

6. Ask students to record their improvised solos and save their best work in each of the two styles.

## Indicators of Success

■ Students improvise pentatonic melodies in two selected styles.

■ Students use pitches within the B-flat pentatonic scale in their improvisations.

■ Students match the tempo and style of the selected accompaniment in their improvisations.

## Follow-up

■ Have students listen to recorded samples of the two contrasting solos they created in the Procedures. Then have them use a teacher-generated rubric to compare and contrast the two versions as they relate to appropriate rhythm, note selection, and articulation.

*Composing and arranging music within specified guidelines: Students compose short pieces within speci-fied guidelines, demonstrating how the elements of music are used to achieve unity and variety, tension and release, and balance.*

## Objective

- Students will determine an appropriate chord progression to accompany a given melody and create a new melody that will complement that chord progression.

## Materials

- Computers with General MIDI sound generation (internal sound card—Windows; QuickTime Musical Instruments—Macintosh) connected to powered speakers or headphones; or computers connected to General MIDI keyboards with powered speakers or headphones

- Accompaniment software such as *Band-in-a-Box* (Victoria, BC: PG Music) or *Visual Arranger* (Buena Vista, CA: Yamaha Corporation of America)

- Teacher-created melody recorded in an accompaniment software file

- Simple musical examples that illustrate unity and variety (see step 1)

- Audio-playback equipment (optional, for musical examples)

## Prior Knowledge and Experiences

- Students have some experience using the accompaniment software.

- Students have a basic knowledge of chord relationships and the letter name abbreviations for major, minor, and dominant seventh chords.

## Procedures

1. Lead students in a brief discussion about the need for a balance of unity and variety in compositions, pointing out that compositions with too much repetition do not have enough variety and that compositions with too little repetition lack unity. Play simple musical examples to illustrate these ideas. Explain to students that they should work to achieve both unity and variety in the compositions they will be creating by using appropriate amounts of repeated and contrasting ideas.

2. Have students open and listen to the file with the teacher-created melody.

3. Ask students to use a trial-and-error approach to typing in letter names of chords that complement the original melody. Remind them to use chords and chord progressions that repeat but also to use contrasting chords. When a satisfactory chord progression has been determined, have students save their files.

4. Have students erase the teacher-created melody in their files and create a new melody that complements the harmony by recording it from the keyboard. Again, emphasize the use of melody and rhythmic patterns that have a good balance of unity and variety.

5. Ask students to select a performance style (for example, jazz swing, light rock, folk) that they think best presents their new compositions and to save their files.

## Indicators of Success

- Students compose chord progressions that complement the given melody.

- Students create new melodies to complement the harmony (chord progression) they created.

- Students play their compositions in selected performance styles at the workstation.

## Follow-up

- Have class listen to several students' compositions created in the Procedures. Lead a discussion of the use of unity and variety in the chords and melody of each composition.

*Composing and arranging music within specified guidelines: Students compose short pieces within specified guidelines, demonstrating how the elements of music are used to achieve unity and variety, tension and release, and balance.*

## Objective

- Students will compose a two-phrase "question and answer" melody that is appropriate for a given harmonic progression.

## Materials

- Computers with General MIDI sound generation (internal sound card—Windows; QuickTime Musical Instruments—Macintosh) connected to powered speakers or headphones; or computers connected to General MIDI keyboards with powered speakers or headphones

- Notation software such as *Music Time* (Philadelphia: GVOX) or *Print Music* (Eden Prairie, MN: Coda Music Technology)

- Teacher-created, two-staff notation file with a chord progression of two phrases using primary chords in the lower staff [*Note:* One phrase should end in a half cadence to illustrate an incomplete phrase (musical tension); the other should end in a full cadence to illustrate a complete phrase (musical release).]

## Prior Knowledge and Experiences

- Students can identify and notate primary chords.

- Students can analyze the pitches used in notated chords to determine possible pitches for use in composing a melody.

## Procedures

1. Discuss with students the terms *tension* and *release*. Use the following examples: taking a difficult test (tension), followed by receiving a good grade on the test (release); posing a question (tension), followed by an answer (release). Illustrate the musical equivalent of question-answer by playing a phrase ending in a half cadence (question), followed by a phrase ending with a full cadence (answer).

2. Explain to students that in order to show that they can create musical tension and release, you want them to compose a two-phrase melody that uses a "question" phrase followed by an "answer" phrase. Remind them that phrases that do not end on the tonic note of the key sound like questions, and phrases that do end on the tonic note of the key sound like answers. Further, explain that they will need to use pitches that work well with the primary chords you will give them in the notation file.

3. Have students listen to the file with the given harmonic progression. Help them identify the primary chords that are used and identify the pitches that might be used to compose a melody for those chords. Also help them identify the end of the question phrase and the end of the answer phrase.

4. Depending on students' rhythmic abilities, give them appropriate guidelines for using notes of various durations, such as half, quarter, and eighth notes. Have them click in notes on the top staff over the chords on the lower staff. Encourage them to listen often, using repeated attempts until they compose a question phrase and an answer phrase that fit well with the given harmonic progression.

## Indicators of Success

- Students compose an incomplete question phrase followed by a complete answer phrase.

- Students use appropriate pitches with the given harmony and stay within all teacher guidelines.

## Follow-up

- Have students continue creating original melodies with more phrases using new keys with fewer or different guidelines. Ask them to evaluate their compositions for overall musical effect and to explain their thinking and choices.

*Composing and arranging music within specified guidelines:* Students use a variety of traditional and nontraditional sound sources and electronic media when composing and arranging.

## Objective

- Students will compose music using sound effects that convey the mood suggested by a picture of a nature scene.

## Materials

- Computers connected to General MIDI keyboards with powered speakers or headphones

- Sequencing software such as *Musicshop* (Nashville: Opcode Systems) or *Master Tracks Pro* (Philadelphia: GVOX)

- Postcards and magazine pictures of nature scenes such as rivers, trees, ocean, meadow, mountains, or planets

- Teacher-prepared sequencing file that demonstrates a composition similar to what the students will be creating

## Prior Knowledge and Experiences

- Students have some experience with the procedure for selecting instrument tone colors and recording tracks using sequencing software.

- Students have used sound effects and electronic tone colors of the synthesizer.

## Procedures

1. Distribute pictures of nature scenes to groups of two students, being sure that students are not aware of the pictures that the other groups have.

2. Explain to students that they are to create a short piece of music that suggests the mood depicted in the picture they are given. Tell them to use only the sound effects (such as rain, wind, and bird songs) and the electronic instrument tone colors (such as bowed pad, sweep, and atmosphere), not an emulation of traditional wind, string, percussion, or keyboard instruments. Also, tell them to use more than one track to record parts that sound simultaneously.

3. Play the teacher-prepared file and discuss the tone color choices you made and their relationship to a selected picture. Describe the techniques you used to create interest and variety in the piece (such as contrasting tone colors, changing dynamics, repeating and contrasting patterns and sections, and contrasting textures).

4. Allow students ample time to experiment and record their parts. Move among students, asking them to explain their choices and giving them feedback.

5. Display all of the pictures for the class. Have students play their compositions for the class, and ask other students to try to identify which picture each composition depicts. Ask students who composed a given piece to explain their tone color choices and the elements of their music in relation to the given picture.

## Indicators of Success

- Students create compositions with a variety of sound sources.

- Students adequately explain their musical choices.

## Follow-up

- Have students listen to works from the traditional repertoire that used nature scenes as the basis for the composition (for example, works by Debussy, Copland, Smetana, or Holst).

*Composing and arranging music within specified guidelines: Students use a variety of traditional and nontraditional sound sources and electronic media when composing and arranging.*

## Objective

- Students will select instruments to orchestrate a given ensemble composition.

## Materials

- Computers connected to General MIDI keyboards with powered speakers or headphones

- Sequencing software such as *Musicshop* (Nashville: Opcode Systems) or *Master Tracks Pro* (Philadelphia: GVOX)

- Teacher-prepared sequencing files of ensemble music with all of the tracks set to use piano tone color (except percussion tracks)—downloaded from web sites such as Classical Archives (http://www.prs.net); for example, "Serenade no. 13 in G for Strings, 'Eine kleine Nachtmusik,' K.525–1. Allegro," by Mozart, or "The Four Seasons, op. 8 no. 1—La Primavera (Spring), 1. Allegro"

## Prior Knowledge and Experiences

- Students have listened to and discussed orchestrations used in film scores (for example, the music of John Williams or Danny Elfman).

- Students can explain how orchestrations use musical elements to evoke a mood or describe a scene in a movie.

- Students have experience using sequencing software to play music files and selecting instruments for tracks in the sequencing file.

## Procedures

1. Explain to students that they will be using sequencing software to orchestrate a piece of music. Ask them to imagine that they are composers who have just finished composing a piece of music for a movie, but the music is written only for piano. Explain that their task is to decide which instruments should play each of the parts (tracks) in the piano piece so that it can be recorded by an instrumental ensemble.

2. Discuss how instruments might be used to suggest a mood or scene (for example, using trombones and cellos to suggest a dark mood; using flutes and violins to suggest a light, high mood; or using timpani to suggest a strong, forceful mood).

3. Have students work in pairs, first to listen to their piece of music using the piano tone color and then to discuss which instruments might work well to emphasize the mood of the music and explain why.

4. Encourage students to experiment and try several different combinations of instruments, making notes about which combinations were most interesting. Move among students and have them explain their choices.

5. When students have finished, have them play their pieces for the class and explain their choices of instruments.

## Indicators of Success

- Students select instruments for each track of the sequencing file for the given composition and explain the reasons for their instrument choices.

## Follow-up

- Have students bring a recording of a movie sound track to class. Ask them to identify the instruments the composer used and to speculate on why the composer might have used those instruments.

*Composing and arranging music within specific guidelines: Students use a variety of traditional and nontraditional sound sources and electronic media when composing and arranging.*

## Objective

■ Students will create and perform an arrangement with melody and accompaniment using one of ten different given musical styles.

## Materials

■ Computers with CD- or DVD-ROM player connected to powered speakers or headphones

■ *Rock Rap 'n Roll* (Reading, MA: Scott Foresman) software and accompanying teacher's guide

■ Copies of "Careful Listening" worksheet (teacher's guide, blackline master, page 43)

■ Copies of "Song Loops Listening Guide" worksheet (teacher's guide, blackline master, page 42)

■ Copies of blank screen *Rock Rap 'n Roll* template, from the inside back cover of the *Rock Rap 'n Roll* teacher's guide

## Prior Knowledge and Experiences

■ Students are familiar with the basic features of *Rock Rap 'n Roll* software.

■ Students understand the concepts of rhythm, syncopation, improvisation, and layering musical textures.

## Procedures

1. Explain to students that they will be creating their own arrangements with melody and accompaniment using the *Rock Rap 'n Roll* software. Give students time to try out all ten musical styles and tell them to select one style for their arrangement.

2. Have students complete the "Careful Listening" worksheet and the "Song Loops Listening Guide," which contain instrument information that will be useful in creating their accompaniments. Then grade and return the worksheets and guides.

3. Have students listen to each Song Loop for their selected style and make a list of which ones are instrumental (1, 2, 3, 4, 6, 9, 10), and which are vocal (5, 7, 8). Ask them to make notes about musical functions that these loops might serve (for example, #1 is a good introduction, #6 has a good bass line, and #10 has a good ending).

4. Have students create their arrangements of the Song Loops by dragging the Song Loop icons to the blank circles, using a minimum of five loops. Have them write down their Song Loop choices on the blank template inside the back cover of the teacher's guide.

5. Give students time to experiment and improvise with the Mousekickers, Voc-A-Lizer, Pitch 'Em, and Magic Fingers to find melodic and rhythmic patterns that fit well with their accompaniments. Encourage careful listening and precise timing of when each pattern should be played to create satisfying rhythms that fit together well. Discuss the thoughtful use of repetition to create an improvised melody that has unity as well as variety and interest. Ask students to make notes about which patterns they are using and when they will use them.

6. After students have completed their arrangements, give them time to practice. Encourage them to record their performances using the built-in recorder and play them back. Guide students in identifying changes that could improve their arrangements.

7. After students have practiced, have them perform their arrangements live for the class. Lead discussions of strengths and weaknesses in the arrangements.

- Students can identify instrumentation, voices, rhythm, and bass line of a music score.

## Indicators of Success

- Students complete arrangements with melody and accompaniment.
- Students perform their arrangements so that melodic and rhythmic patterns fit well with the accompaniment, use precise timing to create satisfying rhythms, and make thoughtful use of repetition for unity and variety.
- Students describe to the class the strategies they used to determine their choices of melodic and rhythmic patterns.

## Follow up

- Have students listen to recordings of music that use the same musical styles as those in *Rock Rap 'n Roll.* Guide them in discussing the musical choices made by the composers or arrangers.

# STANDARD 5C

*Reading and notating music: Students identify and define standard notation symbols for pitch, rhythm, dynamics, tempo, articulation, and expression.*

## Objective

- Students will design and prepare an interactive computer dictionary of music terminology.

## Materials

- Computers that have microphones, connected to General MIDI keyboards with powered speakers or headphones

- Multimedia software such as *HyperStudio* (Torrance, CA: Knowledge Adventure), *PowerPoint* (Redmond, WA: Microsoft Corporation), or *AppleWorks* (Cupertino, CA: Apple Computer)

- Recorders and classroom percussion instruments (optional)

## Prior Knowledge and Experiences

- Students have experience browsing the Internet and using the selected multimedia software.

- Students have experience using computer drawing, painting, and text tools.

- Students have brainstormed, in groups, to create lists of music terms and symbols for pitch, rhythm, dynamics, tempo, articulation, and expression.

## Procedures

1. Have students, working in groups, select entries for their music dictionaries from their lists of music terms and symbols for pitch, rhythm, dynamics, tempo, articulation, and expression.

2. Instruct groups to prepare definitions for each of their selected entries.

3. Ask each group to arrange its entries alphabetically. Have groups use the selected multimedia software to prepare a slide or "card" for each letter of the alphabet. These slides or cards will serve as dictionary pages to display the definitions.

4. Explain to students that the slide or card for each entry should include (a) the selected term, and (b) a text box with the group's written definition of the term. Discuss with students the various ways that they can complete each entry—for example, recording sound samples of their own singing or playing (on keyboards, recorders, or classroom percussion instruments); or drawing or copying symbols onto the computer page. Explain that they can also choose to record their own reading of any definition.

5. Have groups prepare slides for each of their selected entries, as explained in step 4.

6. Help each group design and create a title-page slide for its dictionary. Explain that this slide should include the title of the dictionary, the names of all students in the group, a music-related graphic, a background color, and hypertext links to each letter of the alphabet.

7. Guide each group in preparing a slide containing an index of its dictionary entries, including hypertext links to the appropriate slides.

## Indicators of Success

- Students accurately define notation symbols for pitch, rhythm, dynamics, tempo, articulation, and expression.

- Students select and record appropriate sound samples for their dictionary entries.

- Students draw or copy appropriate symbols for their dictionary entries.

## Follow-up

■ To make the interactive dictionaries created in the Procedures more informative and musical, have students add appropriate musical excerpts downloaded from the Internet.

■ Have students add to their interactive dictionaries by creating entries on topics such as composers, music history, or music of various world cultures.

■ Give students the opportunity to share their interactive dictionaries with other students and parents at a school open house.

*Reading and notating music: Students use standard notation to record their musical ideas and the musical ideas of others.*

## Objective

- Students will transcribe a melody displayed in a MIDI sequencing program's graphic view into standard notation, demonstrating knowledge of how pitch and duration are notated.

## Materials

- Computers with General MIDI sound generation (internal sound card—Windows; QuickTime Musical Instruments—Macintosh) connected to powered speakers or headphones; or computers connected to General MIDI keyboards with powered speakers or headphones

- Sequencing software such as *Musicshop* (Nashville: Opcode Systems) or *Cakewalk Home Studio* (Cambridge, MA: Cakewalk)

- Teacher-prepared sequencing file with a single-line melody recorded on a track, using rhythm durations with which students are familiar

- Copies of selected melody transcribed into standard notation

- Computer display projector and screen (optional, if there are not enough workstations for students)

- Manuscript paper

## Procedures

1. Review the basic concepts of writing pitches and rhythms in standard notation.

2. Explain to students how to read the graphic (piano roll, iconic) display in a sequencer program. Point out that the vertical axis indicates pitch by showing how high or low the note (icon) is on the grid of lines, and the horizontal axis indicates duration by showing how long or short the note (icon) is. The horizontal grid of lines indicates measures and beats.

3. On the board, demonstrate the procedure students are to follow by transcribing a simple melodic line displayed in graphic (piano roll, iconic) view into standard Western notation.

4. With students working alone or in pairs at workstations, have them open and view the teacher-prepared sequencer file with a recorded melody. Have them transcribe the melody from graphic view to standard notation using manuscript paper. [*Note:* If there are not enough workstations for all students, they can work individually at desks, viewing the sequencer's graphic display from a computer display projector. If there is no computer display projector available, students can work from paper copies that capture a computer screen with a melody displayed in a sequencer's graphic view.]

5. Have students compare their transcriptions to the melody written in standard notation and correct their work as necessary.

6. Discuss with students the similarities between piano roll representations and traditional notation. Emphasize that in both representations the vertical axis indicates higher and lower pitches and the horizontal axis indicates the duration and order of notes.

## Indicators of Success

- Students transcribe a melody displayed in a MIDI sequencing program's graphic view into standard notation.

## Prior Knowledge and Experiences

- Students can notate pitches and rhythms in standard music notation.

## Follow-up

- Have students exchange melodies notated in the Procedures and record the exchanged notated versions into a sequencer using a MIDI keyboard. Ask students to compare the graphic view of this new recording with the original recording's graphic view.

- Ask students to transcribe recorded examples that include various expressive and stylistic markings such as staccato, legato, and rubato. Have students attempt to include these markings appropriately in their transcriptions (for example, notating a passage as quarter notes with staccato marks, instead of eighth notes followed by eighth rests).

*Reading and notating music: Students use standard notation to record their musical ideas and the musical ideas of others.*

## Objective

- Students will transcribe a familiar melody by ear into standard notation.

## Materials

- Computers with General MIDI sound generation (internal sound card—Windows; QuickTime Musical Instruments—Macintosh) connected to powered speakers or headphones; or computers connected to General MIDI keyboards with powered speakers or headphones
- Notation software such as *Music Time* (Philadelphia: GVOX) or *Print Music* (Eden Prairie, MN: Coda Music Technology)

## Prior Knowledge and Experiences

- Students have learned a melody that will be transcribed by singing or playing it on classroom instruments.
- Students can enter and delete pitches and rhythms in notation software using the mouse.
- Students have notated rhythmic and melodic patterns in standard notation.
- Students have used a counting system to count and perform rhythms.

## Procedures

1. Remind students of some of the melodies that they know well, briefly singing or playing the melodies with the students. As they sing, have them indicate melodic contour (intervals) through hand gestures or clap the rhythm of the melodies.

2. Depending on students' skill level, either have them select one of the familiar melodies to transcribe by ear into standard notation using notation software or select a melody for the students.

3. With your help, have students set the meter and key signature for the selected melody. Give them the first pitch and rhythm. Have them use the mouse to click in the next note or notes using the software. To help them determine the pitches, encourage them to think about how the melody is stepping or leaping. Ask them to tap and count the rhythms as a way to choose the correct rhythm value (duration).

4. After students have entered a measure or two, encourage them to sing or hum the melody and listen and compare their notation to what they hear. Have them identify and fix errors, then continue to enter notes and listen again, gradually adding to the notated melody. [*Note:* Some students may want to notate only the rhythm on a single pitch, then go back and drag the notes higher or lower to select the correct pitches.]

5. When students have completed notation of the melody, have them play it with the software and sing or play along with it to demonstrate that their notation is correct.

## Indicators of Success

- Students transcribe a familiar melody by ear into standard notation.

## Follow-up

- Have students transcribe melodies with more difficult rhythms and pitches.
- Have students transcribe a melody and try adding a percussion, chord, or bass part to accompany the melody.

# STANDARD 6A

*Listening to, analyzing, and describing music:* Students describe specific music events in a given aural example, using appropriate terminology.

## Objective

- Students will describe Duke Ellington's use of tone color in his compositions, using appropriate terminology.

## Materials

- Computers that have Internet access and that have powered speakers or headphones
- Web browser software such as *Netscape Communicator* (Mountain View, CA: Netscape) or *Internet Explorer* (Redmond, WA: Microsoft Corporation)
- Software such as *RealPlayer* (Seattle: RealNetworks) that enables user to hear music recordings from the Internet
- Teacher-developed listening sheet (see Listening to Duke Ellington on page 58)

## Prior Knowledge and Experiences

- Students have basic computer skills and are able to find the Duke Ellington web site (http://www.dellington.org) and locate Lesson 1.

## Procedures

1. Introduce Duke Ellington to the class. Explain that Ellington is an African-American composer who led his own jazz orchestra, that he played piano, and that as a young man, he chose to go into music even though he was equally talented as a visual artist. Tell students that today they will learn how Ellington used colors when he composed music. Direct students to Lesson 1 on the Ellington web site (click "Inter-Activities" from home page), "The Color of Ellington's Vision," which contains four pieces for listening and questions about Ellington's creative use of instruments.

2. Guide students to listen to musical examples of Ellington's music and identify instruments used and the mood of each piece on the "Listening to Duke Ellington" worksheet.

3. Have students complete Lesson 1 on the web site.

4. Ask students to proceed to the scrapbook section of the site and find answers to the following questions: What talent did Ellington have other than musical talent? What styles of music were starting to emerge in America? What happened to jazz after World War II?

## Indicators of Success

- Students describe how the blending of instruments creates a musical palette in various Duke Ellington musical examples.

## Follow-up

- Have students view art transparencies from *Duke Ellington Education Kit, Beyond Category* (Parsippany, NJ: Dale Seymour Publications/Pearson Learning, 1997). Lead a discussion about the use of color in art work that Ellington admired. Have students find similarities between these visual art examples and examples of Ellington's music that they have heard.

*(continued)*

# Listening to Duke Ellington

| TITLE | INSTRUMENTS I HEARD | MOOD OF PIECE |
|---|---|---|
| "Black and Tan Fantasy" | | |
| "Creole Love Call" | | |
| "Mood Indigo" | | |
| "Moon Mist" | | |

*Listening to, analyzing, and describing music: Students demonstrate knowledge of the basic principles of meter, rhythm, tonality, intervals, chords, and harmonic progressions in their analyses of music.*

## Objective

- Students will identify the meter signature and tonality for aural examples of familiar songs.

## Materials

- Computers with General MIDI sound generation (internal sound card—Windows; QuickTime Musical Instruments—Macintosh) connected to powered speakers or headphones; or computers connected to General MIDI keyboards with powered speakers or headphones

- Sequencing software such as *Musicshop* (Nashville: Opcode Systems) or *Cakewalk Home Studio* (Cambridge, MA: Cakewalk); or notation software such as *Finale* (Eden Prairie, MN: Coda Music Technology) or *Music Time* (Philadelphia: GVOX)

- Teacher-generated MIDI files of familiar songs that have various meter signatures

- Teacher-generated listening sheet directing students to identify meter signatures for given songs

## Prior Knowledge and Experiences

- Students have sung songs such as "Happy Birthday," "Jingle Bells," or "Oh My Darling Clementine."

- Students have discussed and listened to waltzes, marches, or pop songs in 2/4, 3/4, and 4/4.

## Procedures

1. Play back MIDI files of the selected familiar songs and ask students to identify the meter signature of each song. Then ask them in which meter the song is most often performed.

2. Play MIDI files of the familiar songs in both major and minor keys. [*Note:* Most software programs will allow changing from a major key to a minor key.]

3. Have students identify whether each song is in major or minor and identify in which tonality the songs are most commonly performed.

4. Discuss with students how meter and tonality affect the songs.

## Indicators of Success

- Students identify the meter signature and tonality in examples of familiar songs.

## Follow-up

- Have students create an arrangement of a familiar song, changing tonality and meter to create a new version of the song. [*Note: Band-in-a-Box* (Victoria, BC: PG Music) can be used to change styles from waltz to march and so on and to change tonality easily.]

- Have students listen to *Band-in-a-Box* styles and determine what meter is used for each style.

*Listening to, analyzing, and describing music:* Students demonstrate knowledge of the basic principles of meter, rhythm, tonality, intervals, chords, and harmonic progressions in their analyses of music.

## Objective

■ Students will identify missing primary chords in accompaniments for twelve-bar blues and traditional melodies.

## Materials

■ Computers with General MIDI sound generation (internal sound card—Windows; QuickTime Musical Instruments—Macintosh) connected to powered speakers or headphones; or computers connected to General MIDI keyboards with powered speakers or headphones.

■ Accompaniment software such as *Band-in-a-Box* (Victoria, BC: PG Music) or *Visual Arranger* (Buena Vista, CA: Yamaha Corporation of America)

■ Teacher-generated accompaniment software files with harmonization (primary chords) and recorded melodies for "Things Ain't What They Used to Be" (Duke Ellington)—see chord chart in step 3— and "America, the Beautiful"—see chord chart in step 6 [*Note:* Selected measures should have the chords entered as rests so that they do not sound in the accompaniment (chord letter name followed by period; for example, "F."). These will show on the screen as red letters.]

## Procedures

1. Review with students how to determine the letter names for primary chords in the key of F. Remind students of the order of chords in the twelve-bar blues progression.

2. To help students use the accompaniment software, demonstrate and explain how to find, open, save, and play the files you have created. [*Note:* These can be distributed to students on diskettes or with a network file server.]

3. Open and play the file "Things Ain't What They Used to Be," which has chords entered as follows:

| F | F | F. (rest) | F. (rest) |
|---|---|-----------|-----------|
| I | I | I | I |
| F. (rest) | F. (rest) | F | F |
| IV | IV | I | I |
| F. (rest) | F. (rest) | F | C7 |
| V7 | IV | I | V7 |

Demonstrate the procedure students are to follow by helping them identify and type in the correct letter names to replace names for the first two resting chords (chords not sounding).

4. With students working alone or in pairs, ask them to continue the process of typing in the correct letter names for the resting chords. Encourage them to use what they know about primary chords and to use their ears by listening frequently after they type in letter names. Have students save their version of the file.

5. After students have finished identifying the correct chords, discuss the strategies they used for this process. ("The chords sounded like they fit with the melody." "We knew which chord comes next in the twelve-bar blues progression." "There were only three different chords to try.")

■ "Things Ain't What They Used to Be," in *The Hal Leonard Real Jazz Book* (Milwaukee, WI: Hal Leonard Corporation, 1997)

## Prior Knowledge and Experiences

■ Students have studied primary chords (I—tonic, IV—subdominant, and V7—dominant) and can determine the letter names for these chords in a given key.

■ Students can identify the order of chords in the twelve-bar blues progression.

■ Students have sung or listened to "Things Ain't What They Used to Be" and "America the Beautiful."

6. Have students open and listen to the file for "America, the Beautiful," which has chords entered as follows:

| | | | | |
|---|---|---|---|---|
| C | G7 | C. (rest) | C | |
| C | C. (rest) | A7 | D7 | G7 |
| C. (rest) | C. (rest) | G7 | C | C7 |
| C. (rest) | C | C. (rest) | C | |

Note to students that this melody uses a chord progression that is less predictable than the standard twelve-bar blues progression. Encourage them to use the same procedure and strategies they used earlier to identify and replace letter names for resting chords. Have students save their version of the file.

7. Discuss with students how both melodies used primary chords even though they are in different styles. Explain that many familiar folk, popular, and classical melodies use primary chords for their harmonies.

## Indicators of Success

■ Students identify the correct letter names for the missing primary chords in the two given songs.

■ Students describe the strategies they used to determine the chords.

## Follow-up

■ Have students identify missing chords in the first five phrases of the first movement of Wolfgang Amadeus Mozart's *Eine kleine Nachtmusik,* which will demonstrate the use of primary chords used for a more active melody and harmony in Classical style.

■ Create accompaniment software files with incorrect chords to a given melody, and have students identify and replace the incorrect chords.

■ Have students create their own eight-measure chord progression using primary chords. Then have them use the *Band-in-a-Box* "Wizard" feature to improvise a melody for their chords by tapping keys on the computer keyboard or improvising on a classroom instrument.

# STANDARD 7A

STRATEGY 1 OF 3

*Evaluating music and music performances: Students develop criteria for evaluating the quality and effectiveness of music performances and compositions and apply the criteria in their personal listening and performing.*

## Objective

- Students will distinguish between objective and emotional evaluative criteria, evaluate recorded music using objective criteria that they develop, and explain their evaluations.

## Materials

- Computers that have Internet access

- Printer for computers

- Word processing software with "Save as HTML" feature, such as *AppleWorks* (Cupertino, CA: Apple Computer) or *Microsoft Word* (Redmond, WA: Microsoft Corporation)

- Web page authoring software such as *Netscape Composer* (Mountain View, CA: Netscape) or *Microsoft Front Page Express* (Redmond, WA: Microsoft Corporation)

- Access to an account on a school or commercial World Wide Web server

- One to four recordings of music students have been studying

- Classroom audio-playback equipment or individual tape/CD players with headphones

## Procedures

1. Ask students to name some of their favorite songs and to state why they like those songs. Discuss objective criteria for evaluating music, including evaluating the melody, harmony, rhythm, tone color, and form. Contrast this with emotional criteria for evaluating music, such as the music's association with pleasant experiences, personal feelings, and attraction to performers. Have students discuss a popular song using both emotional and objective criteria.

2. Discuss how professional critics or reviewers of records or movies use a similar process to write reviews published in newspapers and magazines and on the radio, television, or the World Wide Web. Have students read or listen to a review of a recording by a professional reviewer and discuss how the reviewer used objective or emotional criteria.

3. Explain to students that they will be acting as critics or reviewers of recorded music. Tell them that the best reviews will be published on either the class or school web site.

4. Play a recorded selection of your choice for the class, or allow students to choose a selection for listening. As students listen, have them evaluate the work using both the emotional criteria and the objective criteria they have discussed. Have them take notes for use in their written review.

5. Have students write rough drafts of their reviews using word processors. Examine the rough drafts and give feedback to students. Have students revise their evaluations until they are in final form.

6. Have students print their reviews and share them with other class members. Ask students to select the most effective reviews for publication on the class or school web site.

7. Have students whose reviews were selected use the word processor's "Save as HTML" feature to change the word processing file to a web page format. Tell them to open those files in web page authoring software and make any desired changes to the page's layout or appearance. Upload (copy) the pages to the class or school web site, and encourage students to have their peers and families read the reviews.

- Written or aural recording review by a professional reviewer

## Prior Knowledge and Experiences

- Students have basic skills with word processing software and web page authoring software.

## Indicators of Success

- Students write reviews using objective criteria, which they distinguish from emotional criteria.
- Students describe the musical selection in appropriate musical terms and provide clear explanations to support their evaluations of the work.

## Follow-up

- Encourage individual students to write reviews of their favorite recordings on their own for publication on the class or school web site.

*Evaluating music and music performances:* Students develop criteria for evaluating the quality and effectiveness of music performances and compositions and apply the criteria in their personal listening and performing.

## Objective

■ Students will evaluate their arrangements using criteria they develop, offer constructive suggestions for improvement, and revise their arrangements based on the evaluations.

## Materials

■ Computers with CD- or DVD-ROM player connected to powered speakers or headphones

■ *Rock Rap 'n Roll* (Reading, MA: Scott Foresman) software

## Prior Knowledge and Experiences

■ Students have improvised and successfully completed *Rock Rap 'n Roll* arrangements.

## Procedures

1. Play the students' previously completed *Rock Rap 'n Roll* arrangements for the class, asking them to notice which seem most effective overall.

2. Ask students which arrangements seemed most effective. Have them explain the characteristics that make these arrangements more effective than others. Lead a discussion until the group has arrived at a set of criteria that describe effective arrangements.

3. Help students use the identified criteria to develop an evaluation form with a rating scale for each criterion, including a place on the form for open-ended constructive suggestions.

4. Have students listen to the arrangements again, this time using the evaluation form to rate the arrangements and give suggestions.

5. Distribute the completed evaluation forms to the appropriate student arrangers and ask them to revise their arrangements based on the ratings and suggestions on the forms.

6. Have students listen to the revised arrangements and discuss areas where improvements have been made.

## Indicators of Success

■ Students develop criteria for evaluating their arrangements.

■ Students evaluate *Rock Rap 'n Roll* arrangements using the criteria they have developed and offer constructive suggestions for improvement.

■ Students revise their arrangements based on the evaluations.

## Follow-up

■ As a way of illustrating the importance of the criteria they have developed for effective arrangements, have students improvise *Rock Rap 'n Roll* arrangements that intentionally do not meet the criteria they developed for effective arrangements.

*Evaluating music and music performances: Students develop criteria for evaluating the quality and effectiveness of music performances and compositions and apply the criteria in their personal listening and performing.*

## Objective

■ Students will develop criteria for evaluating music, differentiating between emotional and objective evaluations of music, and apply the criteria to selected musical examples.

## Materials

■ Computers that have Internet access

■ Printer for computers

■ Spreadsheet software such as *AppleWorks* (Cupertino, CA: Apple Computer), *Microsoft Works* (Redmond, WA: Microsoft Corporation), or *Microsoft Excel* (Redmond, WA: Microsoft Corporation)

■ Six to eight recordings of music that students have been studying

■ Classroom audio-playback equipment or individual tape/CD players with headphones

## Prior Knowledge and Experiences

■ Students have basic computer skills.

## Procedures

1. Lead the class in generating a list of criteria for the objective evaluation of music. Discuss the difference between objective and emotional criteria. On their individual papers, have students write the criteria across the top. Down the left-hand side of the paper, have students list the six to eight recordings that you have selected.

2. Play the selections for the students. After each selection, allow students to discuss the piece in groups of two or three and rate it on a scale of 1–10 according to each criterion.

3. Using a computer, demonstrate the creation of a spreadsheet file based on the ratings listed by the students. Row 1 should contain the students' criteria. Column A should contain the names of the selections evaluated. Demonstrate how to enter data, total the scores, average the scores, and sort the selections (rows) based on average scores.

4. In groups of two or three, have students create spreadsheets, entering their scores, and using the total and average functions.

5. Have students sort the selections based on total scores, average scores, and different criteria to see which selection scored highest in each area.

6. Ask students to use their spreadsheets to create graphs on the basis of average scores and selected criteria.

7. Have each group print and report its findings, explaining which received the highest scores and the rationale behind the scores. Explain that a student's favorite composition does not necessarily need to correspond to the highest rated work. For example, a student may discover through this process that he or she prefers atonal works to works with a strong tonal center, although an atonal piece would likely score lower in this process. Encourage the student to explain such discrepancies.

*(continued)*

## Indicators of Success

- Students develop objective criteria for evaluating music.
- Students rate several compositions on their criteria and enter their ratings on a spreadsheet.
- Students use their spreadsheets to support their ratings of their selections.

## Follow-up

- Have students bring in a favorite musical selection from any genre, play a portion of it for the class, and review the selection based on the criteria created by the class.

# STANDARD 7B

*Evaluating music and music performances: Students evaluate the quality and effectiveness of their own and others' performances, compositions, arrangements, and improvisations by applying specific criteria appropriate for the style of the music and offer constructive suggestions for improvement.*

## Objective

- Students will evaluate music compositions and offer constructive suggestions for improvement.

## Materials

- Computers that have Internet access
- E-mail software
- E-mail mailing list (listserv) for class and for partner teachers and their students [*Note:* Services for mailing lists are available free from companies such as Yahoo Groups (http://www.yahoo.com).]
- Recording of a selected composition (see step 3)
- Audio-playback equipment

## Prior Knowledge and Experiences

- Students have experience using e-mail.
- Students have experience analyzing and describing music.

## Other Requirements

- Agreement with one or two other music teachers in another location to have classes participate in a joint online discussion group to analyze and evaluate a given composition, preferably using the same recording
- Consensus with offsite teacher(s) on project parameters and goals [*Note:* This agreement might be established using a music education listserv such as ArtsEdge (http://artsedge. kennedy-center.org).]

## Procedures

1. Work with students to create specific criteria for evaluating the quality and effectiveness of compositions that they have been listening to or performing. Using the mailing list (listserv), have students send the criteria to the partner students and teachers for discussion.

2. After feedback from the partners, have students create and send a revised list of criteria to be used by students for future evaluations.

3. Ask students, in groups of four or five, to use the criteria they have developed to evaluate the composition agreed upon with the offsite teachers (see Other Requirements above). Have them write constructive suggestions for improvement. Share these group evaluations with the mailing list.

4. Engage the students in discussing the differences and similarities between the various responses. Discuss how many aspects of music may be interpreted in various ways and explain that different people may not come to the same conclusion.

## Indicators of Success

- Students critically evaluate a given musical composition.
- Students describe in their evaluations aspects of the music that might not be apparent to the casual listener.
- Students make insightful, thoughtful, and appropriate comments about a composition and offer constructive suggestions for improvement.
- Students demonstrate a tolerance and understanding of other viewpoints in their analyses of music.

## Follow-up

- Pair students with other students from the partner schools in order to work on similar evaluations, making sure that the same recordings are available to each student.
- Ask students to submit to the mailing list their own reviews of music and performances they have heard outside of class.
- Have students share with their partner schools descriptions of music they have heard in their community.

*Understanding relationships between music, the other arts, and disciplines outside the arts: Students compare in two or more arts how the characteristic materials of each art can be used to transform similar events, scenes, emotions, or ideas into works of art.*

## Objective

- Students will compose a piece of music, or a soundscape, based upon colors and movement found in a work of abstract art.

## Materials

- General MIDI keyboards
- At least two pieces of contrasting abstract art: one with predominantly cool colors (such as Georgia O'Keeffe's "Jack in the Pulpit" series) and one with warm colors (such as Mark Rothko's "Orange and Tan"), both available at the National Gallery of Art web site (http://www.nga.gov)
- Recording equipment
- Headphones (optional)

## Prior Knowledge and Experiences

- Students have studied the concept of warm and cool colors.
- Students can identify samples of color palettes and sort colors appropriately into warm and cool colors.
- Students can identify movement or structure of an artwork.
- Students have studied the concepts of range, timbre, and sound envelope (variation in pitch, amplitude, or timbre over the duration of each tone).

## Procedures

1. Play various timbres on the keyboard and have students decide whether the sounds are warm or cool. Remind students that one person's perception may not match another's, but that certain similarities exist. Create a classification table on the board. Guide students with questions such as these: Does the range of the sound make a difference in its perceived color? What makes a timbre sound warm or cool? Does loudness make a difference?

2. Play various timbres on the keyboard and have students discover and describe any movement within the timbres. Ask, "Do some sound envelopes create a sense of movement (either up, down, or the same)?" Create a list on the board of short vs. long envelopes, and of any special effects envelopes that move (such as applause) when played in certain ways.

3. Help students examine two contrasting abstract artworks that are in opposite color schemes. Discuss the similarities and differences of the music timbres and sound envelopes compared with the colors and movement of the images.

4. Divide the class into groups. Have the groups use the lists on the board to create a soundscape that reflects one of the artworks. Set a minimum and maximum time for length, such as sixty to ninety seconds of sound.

5. Have the groups perform and record their compositions. Play a guessing game to see whether the students can identify which artwork inspired which composition. [*Note:* If class is working as a single group, have other classes do the guessing.]

## Indicators of Success

- Student create soundscapes reflecting the color and movement of an artwork.
- Students describe the sound choices in their compositions by comparing their choices to the artwork.
- Students correctly identify other groups' reflections of artworks.

## Follow-up

- Have students create an artwork based on an abstract piece of twentieth-century music, such as Berio's "Visage" or Varèse's "Poème Electronique."

*Understanding relationships between music, the other arts, and disciplines outside the arts: Students compare in two or more arts how the characteristic materials of each art can be used to transform similar events, scenes, emotions, or ideas into works of art.*

## Objective

- Students will create a web page that relates the artistic contributions made in music and visual art during the early 1900s in Paris to each other and to social events and intellectual ideas during the same period.

## Materials

- Computers that have Internet access and that have General MIDI sound generation (internal sound card—Windows; QuickTime Musical Instruments—Macintosh) connected to powered speakers or headphones

- Web page authoring software such as *Netscape Composer* (Mountain View, CA: Netscape) or *Microsoft Front Page Express* (Redmond, WA: Microsoft Corporation)

- Template for web page layout

- Web browser software such as *Netscape Communicator* (Mountain View, CA: Netscape) or *Internet Explorer* (Redmond, WA: Microsoft Corporation), configured with bookmarks for Impressionist web sites—for example, ArtCyclopedia (http://www.artcyclopedia.com/history/impressionism.html) and the web page template— (see step 4)

## Procedures

1. Divide the class into groups and tell the groups to follow the Internet Scavenger Hunt handout to discover on bookmarked web sites facts about composers and artists of the Impressionist period, such as the composers Debussy, Ravel, and Stravinsky and the artists Picasso, Monet, and Degas.

2. Tell students to listen to the selected compositions and describe on the handout what they hear. Also, ask them to record the URLs they use since they will be returning to the sites to download files later.

3. Have the groups follow the handout to view representative works of art and describe on the handout what they see. Remind them to record the URLs of the sites they use.

4. Ask the groups to select and download one composition and one piece of visual art based on similar events, scenes, emotions, or ideas. Tell the groups to import the sound file and image into the web page template.

5. Have each group write and insert into the template a summary that includes a comparison of how the artist and composer used the characteristic materials of their arts (sound in music and visual stimuli in visual art) in their creations.

## Indicators of Success

- Students produce web pages that compare related works of visual art and music.

- Students compare how a composer and an artist used the characteristic materials of their arts in specific works based on similar events, scenes, emotions, or ideas.

*(continued)*

- Copies of teacher-prepared handout ("Internet Scavenger Hunt") listing composers of the Impressionist period (such as Debussy, Ravel, and Stravinsky) and artists of the period (such as Picasso, Monet, and Degas), with space allowed for students to list titles of compositions or paintings, descriptions of what they hear and see, and web site URLs for the source of their information

## Prior Knowledge and Experiences

- Students have experience browsing the Internet and downloading files from it.
- Students have basic word processing skills.

## Follow-up

- Have students post their web pages on the school web site.

# STANDARD 8B

*Understanding relationships between music, the other arts, and disciplines outside the arts: Students describe ways in which the principles and subject matter of other disciplines taught in the school are interrelated with those of music.*

## Objective

- Students will combine writing skills and music knowledge to write CD liner notes for their compositions, and describe how the principles of language arts and music are related.

## Materials

- Computers with printer
- Page layout software such as *PageMaker* (San Jose, CA: Adobe Systems), *AppleWorks* (Cupertino, CA: Apple Computer), or *Microsoft Word* (Redmond, WA: Microsoft Corporation)
- Teacher-prepared CD liner template file
- Examples of CD liner notes for music of different genres
- Computer scanner (optional)

## Prior Knowledge and Experiences

- Each student has created three or four compositions.

## Procedures

1. Show the class several different examples of CD liner notes for music of different genres. Discuss how the liner notes reflect the music on the CDs. Ask students to list the elements common to all the liner notes, such as cover art, title, names of musicians, list of contents, and descriptions of the pieces. Tell students that they will be making their own liner notes to showcase their compositions.

2. Divide the class into groups of two or three students. Tell each group to design its liner notes on a sheet of paper, including all the elements listed in step 1.

3. Demonstrate opening the CD template in the page layout program, using clip art and scanned art, creating a title and changing the font and style, and other options. Using the examples of liner notes, discuss how the notes can complement the music.

4. Have the groups work with the page layout template to create and print their liner notes. Ask students to add information about each piece to the interior of the liner notes, writing a short paragraph to describe their inspiration for each piece, the style of each piece, and any other details they wish to add.

5. Discuss with students how the principles of language arts that they applied in this lesson relate to the knowledge of music that they applied. Ask, for example, how their musical skills and knowledge helped them in writing the liner notes or how their skills in language arts helped them in describing their compositions.

## Indicators of Success

- Students create liner notes that contain cover art, title, names of musicians, list of contents, and descriptions of the pieces, including a description of the inspiration for each piece and the style of each piece.
- Students describe the relationship between the principles of language arts and music as they applied them in this lesson.

## Follow-up

- At the end of the term, have students create liner notes featuring their best compositions. Have them record their compositions to produce an audio CD with liner notes for their portfolio.

# STANDARD 9A

*Understanding music in relation to history and culture: Students describe distinguishing characteristics of representative music genres and styles from a variety of cultures.*

## Objective

- Students collaborating from classrooms at two different sites will describe distinguishing characteristics of music representing a specific genre, style, or culture.

## Materials

- Computers that have Internet access and video-in capability, connected to powered speakers and e-mail

- Video camera connected to video-in of computer

- Video teleconferencing software such as *CU-See-Me* (Nashua, NH: CUseeMe Networks) or *Microsoft Netmeeting* (Redmond, WA: Microsoft Corporation)

- Composer-related library resources and CDs

- CD players

- Computer display projector and screen

- List of composers

- Copies of assessment handout (see step 6)

## Prior Knowledge and Experiences

- Students have experience using library resources and writing and presenting reports.

## Procedures

1. Connect the computers in both classrooms to the Internet, project the images onto the screens, and establish contact between the classrooms through the video teleconferencing software.

2. Present the parameters of the research project to the students. Introduce pairs of students (one from each site) who will collaborate to research the biography and one composition of a composer from the given list.

3. Guide students in the preparation of their outlines, listening lessons, and the format of their reports as they communicate with their partners daily for two weeks. Help them focus on distinguishing characteristics of the music of each composer.

4. Guide student pairs in practicing their presentations via video teleconferencing.

5. Have students present their final projects to both classes, with one student in each pair presenting the oral report and the other presenting the listening lesson.

6. Distribute the assessment handout to all students. Ask students to place the composers in chronological order on the handout and recap information related to each composer and composition, focusing on distinguishing characteristics.

## Indicators of Success

- Students aurally identify the composer and literature examples when the teachers present segments of the listening lessons.

- Students identify distinguishing characteristics of music by the selected composer.

- Students have experience using e-mail.

## Other Requirements

- Agreement with a music teacher in another location to have classes collaborate on researching given compositions and presenting reports via video teleconferencing

- Consensus with offsite teacher on project parameters and goals

## Follow-up

- Present segments of the listening lessons from the Procedures, and have students identify the composer and literature examples.

- Provide additional examples of listening lessons from the list of composers, asking students to compare and contrast characteristics with the examples used in the Procedures.

*Understanding music in relation to history and culture: Students classify by genre and style (and if applicable, by historical period, composer, and title) a varied body of exemplary (that is, high-quality and characteristic) musical works and explain the characteristics that cause each work to be considered exemplary.*

## Objective

- Students describe the special characteristics that make the music of Claude Debussy exemplary.

## Materials

- Computers that have Internet access and General MIDI sound generation (internal sound card—Windows; QuickTime Musical Instruments—Macintosh) connected to powered speakers or headphones

- Web browser software such as *Netscape Communicator* (Mountain View, CA: Netscape) or *Internet Explorer* (Redmond, WA: Microsoft Corporation)

- Copy of the "Debussy Scavenger Hunt" worksheet (see page 75) for each student

## Prior Knowledge and Experiences

- Students have studied Debussy and his music in previous lessons.

## Procedures

1. Ask students to name some of their favorite music artists and discuss how those artists' personal lives have influenced their music. Explain that knowing about a composer's life can make his or her music more meaningful for the listener. Tell students that today they will learn more about the life of Claude Debussy, how his life influenced his music, and what makes his work exemplary.

2. Show students how to access the Internet and select the bookmark for "Claude Debussy — The Musical Impressions" (http://public.srce.hr/~fsupek/index.html), including how to use the site's internal links.

3. Divide the class into groups of two or three students and distribute the "Debussy Scavenger Hunt" worksheet. Ask each group to explore the web site using the worksheet.

4. Discuss the groups' responses on the worksheet with the class, including information about the *Children's Corner* suite and "Prelude to the Afternoon of a Faun." Guide them in describing the characteristics that make these compositions exemplary.

## Indicators of Success

- Students describe the relationship between Debussy's life and the style of his music.

- Students describe the characteristics that make *Children's Corner* suite and "Prelude to the Afternoon of a Faun" exemplary.

## Follow-up

- Have students find out three interesting events in the life of another composer of their choice, using the Internet, books, magazines, or other resources, and to listen to music of that composer. Ask them to share this information with the class and discuss possible ways that these events may have impacted each composer's music.

# Debussy Scavenger Hunt Worksheet

Go to "Claude Debussy—The Musical Impressions"
   (http://public.srce.hr/~fsupek/index.html).

1. In the photo gallery, what is the name of the little girl with whom Debussy is pictured?

2. What is the little girl's full name and how is she related to Debussy?

3. What piece of music did Debussy dedicate to her?

4. List the movements of this work.

5. Which movement can you listen to on this site?

6. Listen to this movement and describe what you hear. What characteristics of the music make it high quality and exemplary?

7. Listen to "Prelude to the Afternoon of a Faun" and describe what you hear. What characteristics of the music make it high quality and exemplary?

8. What other work inspired "Prelude to the Afternoon of a Faun"?

9. What is "La boîte à joujoux?"

10. What is on the cover of the original edition of "La boîte à joujoux?"

*Understanding music in relation to history and culture: Students classify by genre and style (and if applicable, by historical period, composer, and title) a varied body of exemplary (that is, high-quality and characteristic) musical works and explain the characteristics that cause each work to be considered exemplary.*

## Objective

- Students will identify characteristics that make a given work exemplary using online resources.

## Materials

- Computers that have Internet access
- Web browser software such as *Netscape Communicator* (Mountain View, CA: Netscape) or *Internet Explorer* (Redmond, WA: Microsoft Corporation)
- Teacher-prepared WebQuest-type exploration (see http://edweb.sdsu.edu/webquest/)
- Hot list of sites, related to a teacher-selected work for study, created at Filamentality (http://www.kn.pacbell.com) —see step 1
- List of composers

## Prior Knowledge and Experiences

- Students have experience using a web browser.

## Procedures

1. Have pairs of students access the hot list you created at Filamentality and visit sites to discover information on the musical work that you have identified. Ask each pair to research specific items related to the composition, including what makes it exemplary, when it was written, biographical information on the composer, recorded performances, the elements that define the piece as being in a particular style, and instrumentation.

2. Ask students to present what they have learned to the class. Lead a discussion about what makes the work exemplary.

3. Have pairs of students choose another composer from the list you have prepared. Ask them to use the Internet to find a famous composition by the composer and gather specific items about the composer and composition, including what makes the composition exemplary. Tell them to write down the URLs of the related links.

4. Ask students to use Filamentality to create their own hot lists containing the links related to a composer and comments about the information in the links.

5. Have groups display their web pages to each other, playing and discussing the compositions.

## Indicators of Success

- Students develop hot lists of sites related to a particular composer.
- Students identify characteristics that cause given works to be exemplary.

## Follow-up

- Post web pages students have created to the school's web site. Have students write their own descriptions of compositions and link them to other students' web pages.

# STANDARD 9C

*Understanding music in relation to history and culture:* Students compare, in several cultures of the world, functions music serves, roles of musicians, and conditions under which music is typically performed.

## Objective

- Students will develop brochures describing music of a specific culture, functions the music serves, roles of musicians, and conditions under which the music is typically performed.

## Materials

- Computers with printer
- Page layout software such as *PageMaker* (San Jose, CA: Adobe Systems), *AppleWorks* (Cupertino, CA: Apple Computer), or *Microsoft Word* (Redmond, WA: Microsoft Corporation)
- Variety of books on music and musicians and CD-ROM encyclopedia
- List of links to culture-specific web sites
- Teacher-generated project instruction sheet, including rubric for assessing students' work
- Copies of sample brochure

## Prior Knowledge and Experiences

- Students have experience browsing the Internet.
- Students have basic word processing skills.

## Procedures

1. Divide the class into groups according to the number of cultures being studied.

2. Distribute and discuss the project instruction sheet. Discuss with students how they can use books on music and musicians, the CD-ROM encyclopedia, and links to culture-specific web sites to find information on music of a specific culture, including functions the music serves, roles of musicians, and conditions under which the music is typically performed.

3. After students have completed some of their research, pass out a sample brochure and discuss instructions about how to create a brochure.

4. When students have finished creating their brochures, discuss the rubric on the instruction sheet and have them assess their work using the rubric.

5. Have students print their brochures and post them in the classroom.

## Indicators of Success

- Students develop brochures describing the music of a specific culture, functions the music serves, roles of musicians, and conditions under which the music is typically performed.
- Students assess their own work using a given rubric.

## Follow-up

- Have students export the brochures they have created as HTML files and post them on the school's web site. Enlarge the brochures to decorate the room for a concert of multicultural music.

# PERFORMING ENSEMBLES
## Grades 5–8

# STANDARD 1C

*Singing, alone and with others, a varied repertoire of music:* Students sing music representing diverse genres and cultures, with expression appropriate for the work being performed.

## Objective

- Students will sing and play a melody from an instrumental setting of a folk song with proper phrasing and expression.

## Materials

- Computer that has Internet access; printer for computers

- Web browser software such as *Netscape Communicator* (Mountain View, CA: Netscape) or *Internet Explorer* (Redmond, WA: Microsoft Corporation)

- Notation software such as *Finale* (Eden Prairie, MN: Coda Music Technology) or *Sibelius* (Cambridge, England: The Sibelius Group)

- Score and parts from an instrumental setting of folk songs, such as *Fantasy on a Canadian Folk Song* by Mike Hannickel ("Donkey Riding")(Lexington, KY: Curnow Music Press); and *English Folk-Song Fantasy* by Frank Erickson ("Morning Dew" "My Bonny, Bonny Boy," and "Seventeen Come Sunday")(Van Nuys, CA: Alfred Publishing Company)

- Notation (teacher-notated using notation software) for one of the folk melodies, including lyrics and needed transpositions

## Prior Knowledge and Experiences

- Students have been rehearsing the selected folk-song setting.

## Procedures

1. During the warm-up period, distribute the transposed parts for the selected folk melody. Sing the melody for students, emphasizing phrasing and demonstrating conducting.

2. Have sections of the ensemble take turns playing and singing the melody with correct phrasing; for example, brasses sing while woodwinds play.

3. Involve students in a discussion of the meaning of the lyrics.

4. Ask for volunteers to play or sing the melody with dynamics that express the mood of the text.

5. Have students select the most effective sung and played demonstrations of the melody. Ask ensemble to sing the melody in unison, emphasizing proper phrasing and expression.

## Indicators of Success

- Students sing and play the folk melody in unison with proper phrasing and expression.

## Follow-up

- Have ensemble play sections of the instrumental setting used in the Procedures, applying what they learned about proper phrasing and expression in singing the folk song.

*Choral*

# STANDARD 1D

**STRATEGY 1 OF 2**

*Singing, alone and with others, a varied repertoire of music:* Students sing music written in two and three parts.

## Objective

- Students will sing their parts in a two- or three-part choral composition.

## Materials

- Computers with General MIDI sound generation (internal sound card—Windows; QuickTime Musical Instruments—Macintosh) connected to powered speakers or headphones; or computers connected to General MIDI keyboards with powered speakers or headphones

- Sequencing software such as *Musicshop* (Nashville: Opcode Systems) or *Cakewalk Home Studio* (Cambridge, MA: Cakewalk); or notation software such as *Encore* (Philadelphia: GVOX) or *Sibelius* (Cambridge, England: The Sibelius Group)

- Two- or three-part choral arrangement

- Teacher-prepared multi-track sequence of vocal parts and the accompaniment of the selected choral arrangement [*Note:* Each vocal part is recorded on its own track, using a different instrument sound for each part.]

- Computer display projector and screen (optional)

## Prior Knowledge and Experiences

- Students can visually track a unison score.

## Procedures

1. Explain that each vocal part of the selected choral arrangement has been assigned a different instrument sound on the sequence. Play back a few measures of each vocal track (soloed) so that students may identify the timbre of their parts.

2. If display projector is used, play all parts simultaneously as students listen for their vocal parts and follow notation on the screen.

3. Play all parts simultaneously as students listen for and follow their ensemble parts in their choral octavos.

4. Play all parts simultaneously as students sing their parts along with the MIDI sequence.

## Indicators of Success

- Students sing a two- or three-part choral piece accurately, in tune, and with rhythmic precision.

## Follow-up

- Have students rehearse their parts for the choral arrangement used in the Procedures, either individually or in small groups with the sequence in a practice room, muting and soloing tracks as needed.

*Singing, alone and with others, a varied repertoire of music: Students sing music written in two and three parts.*

## Objective

- Students will use a four-track recorder to record themselves singing each part of a two-part composition.

## Materials

- Four-track recorder with speakers and microphone
- Two-part choral composition
- Audiocassette tape of accompaniment for the selected choral composition
- Audiocassette tape recorder
- Copies of teacher-generated handouts explaining how to dub cassette onto four-track tape and how to record vocal tracks

## Prior Knowledge and Experiences

- Students have been rehearsing their parts in the selected two-part choral composition.

## Procedures

1. Demonstrate how to dub cassette onto four-track tape and how to record vocal tracks.

2. Distribute the handouts and have students follow them to dub the audiocassette tape of the accompaniment for the selected choral composition onto four-track tape.

3. As students sing their parts, have them record each part of the two-part composition, first recording one part on one of the remaining tracks, then rewinding and recording the other vocal part on the remaining track.

## Indicators of Success

- Students sing their parts of the two-part composition accurately and with good breath support.

## Follow-up

- Have students use an effects box with the four-track recorder to add reverb or other effects to tracks.

# STANDARD 1E

*Singing, alone and with others, a varied repertoire of music:* Students sing with expression and technical accuracy a varied repertoire of vocal literature with a level of difficulty of 3, on a scale of 1 to 6, including some songs performed from memory.

## Objective

- Students will individually perform, from memory and with accompaniment, a vocal part in literature with a level of difficulty of 3 and evaluate their expression and technical accuracy.

## Materials

- Computers with microphones, connected to General MIDI keyboards, with powered speakers or headphones

- Sequencing software with digital audio such as *Cakewalk Home Studio* (Cambridge, MA: Cakewalk), *Metro 5* (Cambridge, MA: Cakewalk), or *MicroLogic AV* (Grass Valley, CA: Emagic Soft- und Hardware GmbH/Emagic, Inc.)

- Choral work with a level of difficulty of 3

- Teacher-prepared MIDI sequence of the accompaniment to the selected choral work [*Note:* Save the sequence as read-only.]

- Copies of teacher-prepared handout with self-evaluation rubric for selected work

## Prior Knowledge and Experiences

- Students have rehearsed and memorized the selected choral work.

## Procedures

1. Have individual students go to a practice room to open the MIDI sequence of the accompaniment for the selected choral work and save a copy of it, renamed with their initials and the date (for example, KCW052201).

2. Ask students to select a digital audio track, click the record button, sing their vocal parts with expression and technical accuracy along with the accompaniment tracks, and save the file again.

3. In class, distribute the handout with the self-evaluation rubric. Have students play back their recordings and, using the rubric, evaluate their performances in regard to expression and technical accuracy.

## Indicators of Success

- Students sing their vocal parts from memory with expression and technical accuracy.

- Students evaluate their performances using the given rubric.

## Follow-up

- Distribute and discuss the evaluations created in step 3 of the Procedures. Have small groups of students record themselves and evaluate their group performances of the selected choral work.

***Performing on instruments, alone and with others, a varied repertoire of music:*** *Students perform on at least one instrument accurately and independently, alone and in small and large ensembles, with good posture, good playing position, and good breath, bow, or stick control.*

## Objective

- Students will perform on percussion instruments with rhythmic accuracy, correct playing position, and good stick control.

## Materials

- Computers with General MIDI sound generation (internal sound card—Windows; QuickTime Musical Instruments—Macintosh) connected to powered speakers or headphones

- *Rhythm Tutor* (Palo Alto, CA: Copperman Software Products) software with exercises identified that include rhythms to be used in the music the ensemble is studying

- Ensemble music with specific rhythm challenges for percussionists (for example, triplets, syncopated rhythms)

## Prior Knowledge and Experiences

- Students can accurately count rhythms to be used in this lesson.

- Students have experience using the *Rhythm Tutor* software.

## Procedures

1. Review counting of the rhythms to be rehearsed in this lesson.

2. Direct students to work on specific exercises using *Rhythm Tutor*. Remind them to use correct playing position and good stick control.

3. When the scores students receive for their playing in *Rhythm Tutor* consistently indicate correct playing, have students apply their learning to ensemble music. Direct students in a performance of the ensemble music, having them focus on accurate playing of the rhythms they have been practicing, as well as correct playing position and good stick control.

## Indicators of Success

- Students accurately perform rhythm exercises in the selected ensemble music.

- Students perform with correct playing position and good stick control.

## Follow-up

- In a sequencing program such as *Musicshop* (Nashville: Opcode Systems) or *Master Tracks Pro* (Philadelphia: GVOX), have percussionists create a drum accompaniment to a teacher-generated MIDI song. To help students focus on creating drum parts in tempo, have them use a metronome sound during recording.

*Performing on instruments, alone and with others, a varied repertoire of music:* Students perform on at least one instrument accurately and independently, alone and in small and large ensembles, with good posture, good playing position, and good breath, bow, or stick control.

## Objective

- Students will accurately perform selected solos of their choice, using good posture, correct playing position, and good breath, bow, or stick control.

## Materials

- Computers connected to powered speakers or headphones
- *Smart Music* accompaniment software (Eden Prairie, MN: Coda Music Technology) with microphone (footswitch optional)
- Printed music for selected solos (see Prior Knowledge and Experiences)
- "Solo Performance Assessment" sheet (see page 87)
- Video camera and playback equipment

## Prior Knowledge and Experiences

- Students have been studying their instruments for at least one year.
- Students have experience operating a workstation equipped with *Smart Music*.
- Students have each selected and printed out a solo from the beginning-level solos available in *Smart Music*.

## Procedures

1. Direct students to practice their selected solos, experimenting with a variety of tempos and choosing an appropriate tempo for their solo performances. Remind them to perform accurately and to use good posture, correct playing position, and good breath, bow, or stick control.

2. Have students perform their solos for the class along with the *Smart Music* accompaniment. Videotape each student performance.

3. Play back the videotapes for the class. Have each student in the class evaluate his or her performance by filling out a "Solo Performance Assessment" sheet.

## Indicators of Success

- Students perform their selected solos with accurate playing, good posture, correct playing position, and good breath, bow, or stick control.
- Students evaluate their own performances using the "Solo Performance Assessment" sheet.

## Follow-up

- Have students perform their solos in a concert.

# Solo Performance Assessment

Name: _____ Date: _____

Music Performed: _____

Condition (sight read, rehearsed, taped): _____

Discuss the following performance elements:

| | |
|---|---|
| **POSTURE** | |
| **PLAYING POSITION** | |
| **BREATH, BOW, OR STICK CONTROL** | |

Adapted from *Tools for Powerful Student Evaluation* by Susan R. Farrell (Fort Lauderdale, FL: Meredith Music Publications, 1997), p. 41.

# STANDARD 2B

***Performing on instruments, alone and with others, a varied repertoire of music:** Students perform with expression and technical accuracy on at least one string, wind, percussion, or classroom instrument a repertoire of instrumental literature with a level of difficulty of 2, on a scale of 1 to 6.*

## Objective

- Students will play their parts in a Level 2 ensemble piece, along with a sequenced accompaniment, with technical accuracy and musical expression.

## Materials

- Computers with General MIDI sound generation (internal sound card—Windows; QuickTime Musical Instruments—Macintosh) connected to powered speakers or headphones; or computers connected to General MIDI keyboards with powered speakers or headphones

- Sequencing software such as *Musicshop* (Nashville: Opcode Systems) or *Cakewalk Home Studio* (Cambridge, MA: Cakewalk)

- Sequenced music selection with a level of difficulty of 2

- Audiocassette recorder, microphone, and blank tapes

## Prior Knowledge and Experiences

- Students have experience operating the basic functions of sequencing software, including using transport controls, muting and soloing a track, and changing tempo.

- Students have been rehearsing the music selection.

## Procedures

1. Have students open the MIDI file of their ensemble parts for the musical selection.

2. Review and demonstrate practice techniques with a sequencer, including slowing the tempo, soloing and listening to the individual part, muting the part and practicing, looping short phrases for repeated practice, and playing or singing along with the part and ensemble to check for accuracy. Discuss how students can use this technology to help them improve technical accuracy and expressiveness of their playing.

3. Have students practice their parts individually with the sequencer. Remind them to work on technical accuracy by practicing at a slow tempo and to increase tempo gradually until they reach the target tempo.

4. Ask students to identify places in the music where dynamics change and practice playing with appropriate dynamics.

5. Have students record their parts to cassette tape, focusing on technical accuracy and expressiveness.

6. Lead the ensemble in an expressive and technically accurate performance of the musical selection.

## Indicators of Success

- Students perform their individual parts expressively and with technical accuracy in an ensemble setting.

## Follow-up

- To help students improve not only their note-reading skills but the accuracy of their playing, have them practice reading notation using *Practica Musica* (Kirkland, WA: Ars Nova Software) software. Also, have them practice, using this software, dictation skills (level easy) that relate to literature they are studying as an ensemble. Then have the ensemble perform the literature with increased technical accuracy.

# STANDARD 3C

***Improvising melodies, variations, and accompaniments:*** *Students improvise short melodies, unaccompanied and over given rhythmic accompaniments, each in a consistent style, meter, and tonality.*

## Objective

- Students will improvise melodic responses to "calls" in a major key.

## Materials

- Computers with General MIDI sound generation (internal sound card—Windows; QuickTime Musical Instruments—Macintosh) connected to powered speakers or headphones; or computers connected to General MIDI keyboards with powered speakers or headphones

- *Band-in-a-Box* (Victoria, BC: PG Music) accompaniment software

- *Band-in-a-Box* file with appropriate chords and melodies beginning with OLDMOTWN.STY or CHCLSTRD.STY

- Printed notation with selected "calls" (from the selected *Band-in-a-Box* melodies) transposed for all band members

## Prior Knowledge and Experiences

- Students can play the F concert scale.

- Students can identify scale degrees (tonic, supertonic, etc.) for each note in the F concert scale.

- Students can perform the I, IV, and V chords in the concert key of F. [*Note:* Percussionists should play mallet percussion for this lesson.]

## Procedures

1. In small group or individual lessons, distribute the printed notation for the selected "calls." Using the *Band-in-a-Box* file, have students echo the "call" section of each phrase with the computer-generated accompaniment. Have students improvise "responses" to the calls using the appropriate chord tones.

2. Discuss with students the difference between chord tones, passing tones, and neighbor tones.

3. In performing responses to the calls, have students include chord tones, passing tones, and neighbor tones. Be sure they can identify the types of tones used.

4. Mute the melody track in *Band-in-a-Box* and have one student improvise a new call with other students improvising a response.

5. Repeat step 4 with different students creating the call.

6. Repeat step 4 but with one student creating both the call and the response.

7. Have students experiment with different tempos and styles included with *Band-in-a-Box*. Discuss with students how these changes affect the improvisations.

## Indicators of Success

- Students improvise appropriate call-and-response melodic patterns over the given chord progressions.

## Follow-up

- Have students improvise calls and responses in different keys and styles and of different lengths.

- Have students notate down their favorite "calls" and "responses." Transpose for all band members. Have students perform the new melodies with *Band-in-a-Box* accompaniment at a concert.

# STANDARD 4B

***Composing and arranging music within specified guidelines:*** *Students arrange simple pieces for voices or instruments other than those for which the pieces were written.*

## Objective

- Students will arrange a simple trio for instruments other than those for which the piece was written, using appropriate pitches and ranges.

## Materials

- Computers with General MIDI sound generation (internal sound card—Windows; QuickTime Musical Instruments—Macintosh) connected to powered speakers or headphones; or computers connected to General MIDI keyboards with powered speakers or headphones
- Printer for computer
- Basic notation software such as *Music Time* (Philadelphia: GVOX) or *Print Music* (Eden Prairie, MN: Coda Music Technology)
- *Tunes for Three—Treble Recorder,* arr. Keith Stent (Pacific, MO: Kevin Mayhew Publishers/Mel Bay Publications, 1999); or another collection of instrumental trios

## Prior Knowledge and Experiences

- Students have studied key signatures, meter signatures, and note values.
- Students have basic skills with music notation software.

## Procedures

1. Organize students who play varying instruments into trios or allow students to group themselves. Explain to students that they will be working in their trios to arrange and perform a trio that was originally written for other instruments.

2. Review basic skills in using music notation software to help students set up a three-stave score; enter clefs, key signatures, and meter signatures; add accidentals; and so on.

3. Using the grand staff, review the ranges of the instruments that students play and remind students that they must stay within a comfortable range for their instruments as they arrange the trio.

4. Give students time to select a trio from *Tunes for Three—Treble Recorder.* [*Note:* These trios are printed in concert key.]

5. Have students use notation software to enter the trio they have selected. Encourage them to listen often to "proof hear" and pitch or rhythm entry errors. Have them look for any notes that are too high or low for the instrument that will play a given part. If they find such notes, help them make decisions about possible substitutions. Explain strategies such as transposing up or down an octave, playing unison with another part, and using notes that stay within the harmony. Encourage students to enter dynamics, articulations, accents, and expressions.

6. After students have entered trio scores correctly, explain transposition as needed for B-flat, E-flat, F, or alto clef instruments. Guide students in transposing each staff to the appropriate key. Help them extract and print the transposed individual parts.

7. Give students time to rehearse and then perform their trios.

## Indicators of Success

- Students arrange a trio for their instruments using correct key signatures, pitches, and ranges.

## Follow-up

- Have students compose a fourth instrument part for the arrangements they created in the Procedures.
- Have students compose a percussion part or vocal text for their arrangements.

# STANDARD 5A

***Reading and notating music:*** *Students read whole, half, quarter, eighth, sixteenth, and dotted notes and rests in 2/4, 3/4, 4/4, 6/8, 3/8, and alla breve meter signatures.*

## Objective

- Students will accurately count and play rhythmic phrases using a variety of note and rest values in 2/4, 3/4, 4/4, 6/8, 3/8, and alla breve meter signatures and in various tempos.

## Materials

- Computers with General MIDI sound generation (internal sound card—Windows; QuickTime Musical Instruments—Macintosh) connected to powered speakers or headphones; or computers connected to General MIDI keyboards with powered speakers or headphones

- Accompaniment software such as *Band-in-a-Box* (Victoria, BC: PG Music) or *Visual Arranger* (Buena Vista, CA: Yamaha Corporation of America)

- Teacher-generated accompaniment software files with four-measure chord progression (vamp) accompaniment in an appropriate key (see example in step 2) [*Note:* Set the phrase to repeat from measure one to measure four. Set the number of repetitions ("choruses") of the chord progression in *Band-in-a-Box* according to class size and how you choose to use the activity.]

## Procedures

1. Review the basic concepts of rhythmic notation, including note values and 2/4, 3/4, 4/4, 6/8, 3/8, and alla breve meter signatures.

2. Select a four-measure rhythmic phrase for students to count and play. Open an accompaniment software file such as the following:

   Chorus:  | c min  | F7  | c min  | F7  |

   Select an appropriate accompaniment style for the meter signature of the rhythmic phrase you have chosen. Play the accompaniment and demonstrate how students are to read and count the rhythmic phrase using a counting system or neutral syllable as they listen to the accompaniment. Stress the importance of following the tempo.

3. After demonstrating, have students listen to the accompaniment and count the rhythmic phrase without your help.

4. Discuss key aspects of a successful performance, including starting on time, maintaining a steady tempo, and using correct counting.

5. Have students perform the example on their own instruments, both individually and as a group.

6. Repeat steps 2–5 several times, using new rhythmic phrases and changing accompaniment styles and tempos.

## Indicators of Success

- Students accurately count and play rhythmic phrases using a variety of note and rest durations in 2/4, 3/4, 4/4, 6/8, 3/8, and alla breve meter signatures.

*(continued)*

- Teacher-generated printed four-measure rhythmic phrases in 2/4, 3/4, 4/4, 6/8, 3/8, and alla breve meter signatures; or published examples such as those found in recent instrumental method books

## Prior Knowledge and Experiences

- Students have studied note values and meter signatures.
- Students can count and chant rhythmic patterns.

## Follow-up

- Using a twelve-bar blues progression as an accompaniment, have individual or small groups of students perform one-, two-, or four-measure rhythmic phrases using either the root note as the chords change or alternating between the root and the third or seventh of the chord as the chords change.

# STANDARD 5A

*Reading and notating music: Students read whole, half, quarter, eighth, sixteenth, and dotted notes and rests in 2/4, 3/4, 4/4, 6/8, 3/8, and alla breve meter signatures.*

## Objective

■ Students will accurately count and perform rhythmic patterns using a variety of note and rest values with increasing fluency.

## Materials

■ Computers with General MIDI sound generation (internal sound card—Windows; QuickTime Musical Instruments—Macintosh) connected to powered speakers or headphones; or computers connected to General MIDI keyboards with powered speakers or headphones

■ Computer-assisted instruction software that includes drill-and-practice exercises on reading and playing rhythmic patterns, such as *Music Ace 2* (Chicago: Harmonic Vision) or *Practica Musica* (Kirkland, WA: Ars Nova Software)

■ Record-keeping sheets

## Prior Knowledge and Experiences

■ Students have studied note values and meter signatures.

■ Students can count and chant rhythmic patterns.

## Procedures

1. Review the basic concepts of rhythmic notation, including note values and meter signatures.

2. Have students open the computer-assisted instruction software and select an appropriate section for practicing rhythm reading and performing (see Materials). [*Note:* Be sure to investigate options the software provides for setting the level of difficulty and other parameters for customizing the exercises appropriately for your students.]

3. Open the appropriate rhythm-reading section and demonstrate any procedures students are to follow that may not be readily apparent in the software.

4. Have students begin to work through the exercises. Encourage them to use the rhythm counting system that you normally use in your classroom. After they have completed several items, discuss key aspects of a successful performance, including starting on time, maintaining a steady tempo, and using correct counting.

5. Allow students to continue working, asking them to complete as many exercises as they can, as accurately as they can. When they finish a set of exercises, have them record their scores on their individual record-keeping sheets, updating the sheets each time to show the improvement in their rhythm-reading and performing skills.

6. Have students select one rhythm to perform for the class, either on their instruments or by counting or singing.

## Indicators of Success

■ Students accurately count and perform rhythmic patterns using a variety of note and rest values with increasing fluency.

## Follow-up

■ Have students write their own four-measure rhythmic phrase, then count or perform it. Ask students to exchange rhythmic phrases with other students and perform the other students' phrases.

# STANDARD 5C

***Reading and notating music:*** *Students identify and define standard notation symbols for pitch, rhythm, dynamics, tempo, articulation, and expression.*

## Objective

- Students will correctly identify letter names of notes on treble, bass, and/or alto clefs with increasing fluency.

## Materials

- Computers with General MIDI sound generation (internal sound card—Windows; QuickTime Musical Instruments—Macintosh) connected to powered speakers or headphones; or computers connected to General MIDI keyboards with powered speakers or headphones

- Computer-assisted instruction software that includes drill-and-practice exercises on identifying letter names of notes, such as *Music Ace* (Chicago: Harmonic Vision), *Music Lessons* (Northfield MN: MiBAC Music Software) or *Note Speller* (Champaign, IL: Electronic Courseware Systems)

- Record-keeping sheets

- Written note-naming test with a variety of individual notes on staves in appropriate clefs for students' instruments or voices, including places for students to write in note names

## Prior Knowledge and Experiences

- Students can name the lines and spaces on the clefs for their own instruments or voices.

## Procedures

1. Review the names of the lines and spaces for the clefs in which students will be working.

2. Have students open the computer-assisted instruction software, select the appropriate section for practicing the identification of letter names of notes, and choose the appropriate clef(s). [*Note:* Be sure to investigate options the software provides for setting the level of difficulty and other parameters to customize the exercises appropriately for your students.]

3. With students working individually, ask them to complete as many exercises as they can, as accurately as they can. Encourage them to listen to the sound of each note in addition to naming the notes correctly. When they finish a set of exercises, have them record their scores on their individual record-keeping sheets, updating the sheets each time to show the improvement in their note-naming skills.

4. Give students the written note-naming test to assess how many notes they can identify correctly in a five-minute period.

## Indicators of Success

- Students correctly identify letter names of notes on treble, bass, and/or alto clefs with increasing fluency.

- Students improve their scores as they repeat the drill-and-practice exercises.

## Follow-up

- Have students call out note letter names as they do fingerings before playing a new piece of music.

- Have choral students sing the names of the notes in their music, using correct pitches.

# STANDARD 7B

*__Evaluating music and music performances:__ Students evaluate the quality and effectiveness of their own and others' performances, compositions, arrangements, and improvisations by applying specific criteria appropriate for the style of the music and offer constructive suggestions for improvement.*

## Objective

- Students will critique their performances of selected passages with a steady beat, appropriate dynamics, and good tone quality, and improve their performance based on their evaluations.

## Materials

- Computer with microphone, connected to powered speakers or headphones

- Basic digital audio-recording software such as *SoundHandle* (freeware) by Dale Veeneman (download from ZDNet— http://www.zdnet.com), or *PeakLE* (Petaluma, CA: BIAS) for Macintosh; or *Sound Recorder* (built into Windows 95/98) or *Sound Forge XP* (Madison, WI: Sonic Foundry) for Windows [*Note:* This type of software records and saves a digital audio file to the hard drive and displays a graphic representation of the waveform of the student's sound.]

## Prior Knowledge and Experiences

- Students have basic skills in performing with a steady beat, appropriate tempo and dynamics, and good tone quality in instrumental performance.

## Procedures

1. For improving performance of steady beat, use the digital audio software to record students playing a passage that calls for a steady beat, especially one that presents a challenge to them.

2. Play back the performances for the students, pointing out the graphic "blocks" in the display of the waveform that represents each separate note played. Then have students join with you in clapping a steady beat along with the recording. Variations in tempo, hesitations, and other errors will become apparent. Discuss these and have students record their passages again.

3. For improving performance of dynamics, record students playing a crescendo while sustaining a single pitch over the course of eight beats at a moderate tempo.

4. Examine the waveform with students and point out that loudness (amplitude) is represented graphically by the waveform's distance above and below the "x" (horizontal) axis. Explain that an ideal *crescendo* will graphically look something like a traditionally notated *crescendo* symbol (following the initial "spike" at the onset of the sound). Discuss the students' performances of the *crescendo*. Then, record the *crescendo* again, encouraging students to achieve a smooth and gradual increase in the loudness of the sound.

5. For improving tone quality, record students playing a passage that presents challenges in maintaining a good tone quality.

6. Closely examine the waveform with students for any clear, well-played note. To do this, select (click and drag over) the waveform area for that note and zoom in (make a larger display) of the selected area until individual cycles of the pitch are discernible. Point out the regular, repetitive nature of the cycles. Zoom out (make a smaller display) and listen with students to the entire passage again.

7. Have students select a note that has some tone-quality problems (such as squeak or harshness) and zoom in to closely examine the waveform cycles. Note the irregular, less-clear repetitions of the waveform (because the spectral make-up, or presence of overtones at varying strengths, is changing rapidly). Discuss techniques to improve tone.

*(continued)*

## Indicators of Success

- Students make recordings to which they and the teacher can clap a steady beat.

- Students perform a gradual *crescendo*, as evidenced graphically by a software waveform display.

- Students recognize good tone quality and use techniques to maintain it.

## Follow-up

- Save the audio files from the Procedures in electronic portfolios of students' playing. Examine the files later with students, and compare them with new recordings to track progress.

# STANDARD 8A

***Understanding relationships between music, the other arts, and disciplines outside the arts:*** *Students compare in two or more arts how the characteristic materials of each art can be used to transform similar events, scenes, emotions, or ideas into works of art.*

## Objective

- Students compare the use of characteristic materials of music and visual arts in works they use in creating a multimedia slide show.

## Materials

- Computers that have Internet access

- Web browser software such as *Netscape Communicator* (Mountain View, CA: Netscape) or *Internet Explorer* (Redmond, WA: Microsoft Corporation) with visual art sites bookmarked, such as the National Gallery of Art (http://www.nga.gov)

- Multimedia software such as *HyperStudio* (Torrance, CA: Knowledge Adventure), *PowerPoint* (Redmond, WA: Microsoft Corporation), or *AppleWorks* (Cupertino, CA: Apple Computer)

- Music the ensemble has been rehearsing

- Copies of teacher-prepared handout with spaces for the name of the assigned composition and information for several examples of visual art (see step 1)

- Computer display projector and screen

- Audio-recording equipment

## Procedures

1. Divide class into groups and assign each group of students a different composition that they have been rehearsing in preparation for a concert. Explain that students should individually browse the Internet for examples of visual art that suggest the mood of a section of their assigned compositions or that reflect similar events, scenes, or ideas.

2. Distribute the handout you have prepared and tell students they should record on the handout the following information about each example: name of the artwork, name of the artist, URL of the web site, and a short statement comparing the way in which the visual artist and the composer have used the characteristic materials of their arts to reflect similar events, scenes, emotions, or ideas.

3. Have groups download their selected artworks to a folder on the computer. Explain that they should note which image should appear at which point in the music by writing on one of their ensemble parts.

4. Tell students to assemble a slide show of the art, using the multimedia software and following the order indicated by their written notes. Explain that each slide should also display the title of the piece, the artist's name, and a statement comparing the way in which the visual artist and the composer used the characteristic materials of their arts to reflect similar events, scenes, emotions, or ideas.

5. In rehearsal, record each of the compositions. Then, have each group present its slide show to the class, advancing slides with the recording.

6. Direct students to write reflections in their portfolios about the aesthetic effect of each multimedia presentation and its effectiveness in using visual artworks that reflect events, scenes, emotions, or ideas similar to those reflected in the music.

*(continued)*

## Prior Knowledge and Experiences

- Students have experience browsing the Internet and downloading images from it.

- Students have been rehearsing the selected compositions (see step 1).

## Indicators of Success

- Students produce and present a multimedia slide show of visual art that reflects events, scenes, emotions, or ideas similar to those reflected in their assigned compositions.

- Students use appropriate terminology for visual art and musical characteristics and elements in writing their reflections.

## Follow-up

- Have students present their multimedia slide shows in a live concert performance of the compositions they have been rehearsing.

# STANDARD 8B

*Understanding relationships between music, the other arts, and disciplines outside the arts:* Students describe ways in which the principles and subject matter of other disciplines taught in the school are interrelated with those of music.

## Objective

- Students will combine reading, writing, and instrumental performance skills to create and perform a story, and describe how the principles of language arts and music are related.

## Materials

- Zeta 5-string Electric Violin
- Zeta Synthony Synthesizer, headphones, and amplified speakers
- Computer
- Printer for computer
- Word processing software such as *AppleWorks* (Cupertino, CA: Apple Computer), *Microsoft Word* (Redmond, WA: Microsoft Corporation), or *WordPerfect* (Ottawa: Corel Corporation)
- Copies of list of sound effects (see step 1)

## Prior Knowledge and Experiences

- Students can play notes on the violin or viola necessary to produce various sound effects.
- Students have the necessary skills for writing a short story.

## Procedures

1. Give each student a list of sound effects that can be produced using the electric violin and synthesizer. Using the electric violin and synthesizer connected to amplified speakers, demonstrate the sound effects.

2. Disconnect the amplifier, and connect headphones to the synthesizer. Let students explore the sound effects independently, using the instrument and headphones.

3. Ask each student to use a word processing program to write a short story (approximately one-and-a-half double-spaced pages) with an active plot. Explain that they should include many opportunities throughout their stories for sound effects that would enhance the story.

4. Direct pairs of students to perform their stories for the class with the electric violin. Explain that one student should read the story with appropriate pauses for sound effects, and the other student should perform the sound effects using the electric violin connected to an amplifier.

5. Discuss with students how the principles of language arts that they applied in this lesson relate to the principles of music that they applied. Ask, for example, how their musical skills and knowledge helped them in writing the story or how the writing of their stories helped them in identifying appropriate sound effects.

## Indicators of Success

- Students combine reading, writing, and instrumental performance skills to create and perform interesting stories.
- Students describe the relationship between the principles of language arts and music as they applied them in this lesson.

## Follow-up

- Have students perform some of the stories with sound effects for parents and guests at a scheduled concert.

# PERFORMING ENSEMBLES
## Grades 9–12

# STANDARD 1B

*Proficient*

**Singing, alone and with others, a varied repertoire of music:** *Students sing music written in four parts, with and without accompaniment.*

## Objective

- Students will sing each part of a four-part chorale with appropriate phrasing and dynamics.

## Materials

- Computer with General MIDI sound generation (internal sound card—Windows; QuickTime Musical Instruments—Macintosh) connected to powered speakers or headphones; or computer connected to General MIDI keyboards with powered speakers or headphones

- Printer for computer

- Notation software such as *Finale* (Eden Prairie, MN: Coda Music Technology) or *Sibelius* (Cambridge, England: The Sibelius Group)

- Parts notated by the teacher, using notation software, for all four parts of a four-part chorale, transposed for each instrument in the ensemble

## Prior Knowledge and Experiences

- Students can read and play simple chorales.

## Procedures

1. During the warm-up period, have students on each part play their parts while other students sing their parts (soprano, alto, tenor, or bass) on a neutral syllable.

2. Use the computer to play the parts while all students sing their own parts. Work with them on appropriate phrasing, dynamics, and balance.

3. Have students play their own parts, applying what they learned in singing the parts to improve phrasing, dynamics, and balance in their instrumental performance.

## Indicators of Success

- Students sing their parts in the chorale with appropriate phrasing, dynamics, and balance.

- Students play their instrumental parts with improved phrasing, dynamics, and balance.

## Follow-up

- Discuss with students how their singing of a chorale helped improve their instrumental performance.

- Have students sightsing another chorale, performing with good balance, phrasing, and interpretation.

# STANDARD 1C

### *Proficient*

***Singing, alone and with others, a varied repertoire of music:*** *Students demonstrate well-developed ensemble skills.*

## Objective

- Students demonstrate well-developed ensemble skills in a joint rehearsal via video conferencing.

## Materials (in each rehearsal room)

- Computers that have Internet access, microphones, and video-in capability, and that are connected to powered speakers

- Video camera connected to video-in of computer

- Video teleconferencing software such as *CU-See-Me* (Nashua, NH: CUseeMe Networks) or *Microsoft Netmeeting* (Redmond, WA: Microsoft Corporation)

- Computer display projector and screen

- Copies of a selected choral work

- Copies of student assessment form

- Piano or amplified keyboard (optional, for accompaniment)

## Prior Knowledge and Experiences

- Students have learned their parts in the selected choral work.

## Other Requirements

- Agreement with music teachers in another location for a rehearsal agenda, including determination of who will be responsible for each aspect of the rehearsal in order to facilitate the rehearsal

## Procedures

1. In each location, start the video teleconferencing software and project image of teacher via the camera, computer, and projector onto the screen. Establish contact between the computers through the Internet, logging in and using software to contact each other.

2. Explain to students that each teacher will contribute to conducting the rehearsal. Conduct a diagnostic/prescriptive joint rehearsal, focusing on ensemble skills such as blend, balance, phrasing, and pronunciation.

3. Have students and teachers at each location take turns performing and critiquing the ensemble at each site.

4. Ask students to complete a written assessment form critiquing the project, critiquing the development of their ensemble skills, and using appropriate music terminology.

## Indicators of Success

- Students demonstrate responsiveness to two different conductors.

- Students demonstrate improved ensemble skills, including improvement in blend and balance.

## Follow-up

- Have schools and communities at each site attend a joint video teleconference performance of the groups, with one teacher conducting and the other narrating.

*Choral*

# STANDARD 1D

*Advanced*

*Singing, alone and with others, a varied repertoire of music:* Students sing with expression and technical accuracy a large and varied repertoire of vocal literature with a level of difficulty of 5, on a scale of 1 to 6.

## Objective

- Students will sing solo vocal literature with a level of difficulty of 5 with expression and technical accuracy and evaluate their performance.

## Materials

- Computers connected to powered speakers or headphones

- *Smart Music* (Eden Prairie, MN: Coda Music Technology) accompaniment software and microphone

- Copies of selected solo vocal literature with a level of difficulty of 5

- *Smart Music* accompaniment file for selected vocal literature

- Previously prepared student-generated vocal solo adjudication form

## Prior Knowledge and Experiences

- Students have experience singing art songs, arias, and show tunes.

- Students have been practicing songs from the repertoire available on the accompaniment disks of the *Smart Music* system. [*Note:* The "automatic accompanist" will follow their tempo much like a live accompanist.]

## Procedures

1. Have each student perform a selected song for the class, using *SmartMusic* as the accompanist. Remind students to give particular attention to expressive singing and technical accuracy.

2. While each student is singing, have the class "adjudicate" the student using the student-generated adjudication form.

3. Discuss the performances, having students give appropriate comments to help each other improve the expression and technical accuracy of their performances.

## Indicators of Success

- Students perform their solos with expression and technical accuracy.

- Students evaluate the performances, giving each other appropriate comments for improving expression and technical accuracy.

## Follow-up

- Have some students perform their solos in a choir concert.

# STANDARD 2A

*Proficient*

*Performing on instruments, alone and with others, a varied repertoire of music: Students perform with expression and technical accuracy a large and varied repertoire of instrumental literature with a level of difficulty of 4, on a scale of 1 to 6.*

## Objective

■ Students will play exercises based on a composition with a level of difficulty of 4, performing with expression and technical accuracy.

## Materials

■ Computer

■ Printer for computer

■ Instrumental literature with a level of difficulty of 4

■ Notation software such as *Finale* (Eden Prairie, MN: Coda Music Technology) or *Sibelius* (Cambridge, England: The Sibelius Group)

■ Teacher-prepared notated exercises [*Note:* To involve all students when some sections need to rehearse a particular portion of the selected literature, prepare three sets of unison exercises (prominent themes, difficult technical passages, and tricky rhythms) based on the composition, and enter them into the music notation program; using the transpose function of the program, prepare exercises for each instrument of the ensemble, then print out and duplicate the parts.]

## Prior Knowledge and Experiences

■ Students have been rehearsing the selected piece.

## Procedures

1. Lead students in playing from the notated "themes" exercises.

2. Ask students to return to the piece they have been rehearsing and identify the instruments that play the themes from the exercises.

3. Lead students in playing from the notated "technical passages" exercises. Rehearse difficult technical passages, keeping all students engaged by breaking passages down and working out problems while all students work on the part.

4. Have students return to the piece after working on each technical passage and identify instruments that play the particular passage.

5. Lead students in playing from the notated "rhythms" exercises. Rehearse tricky rhythms, keeping all students engaged while breaking rhythm problems down and working out counting difficulties.

6. Have students return to the piece after working on rhythms and identify instruments that play the particular rhythms.

7. Continue with other exercises created from the instrumental piece.

## Indicators of Success

■ Students play themes, technically difficult passages, and challenging rhythms with increasing technical accuracy.

■ Students identify music from exercises in the selected instrumental composition and perform their parts in the composition with expression and technical accuracy.

## Follow-up

■ Have students develop unison exercises for other pieces being studied. Help them use the notation software to transpose and print the parts.

*Instrumental*

*Performing on instruments, alone and with others, a varied repertoire of music: Students perform with expression and technical accuracy a large and varied repertoire of instrumental literature with a level of difficulty of 4, on a scale of 1 to 6.*

## Objective

- Students will perform a world music work with a level of difficulty of 4 with expression and technical accuracy and use MIDI wind, percussion, or string controllers to record their performances to existing MIDI files.

## Materials

- Computers connected to General MIDI keyboards or sound module with powered speakers or headphones

- MIDI wind, percussion, or string controllers connected to MIDI IN of MIDI Interface connected to computer

- World music band literature with a level of difficulty of 4, such as "Variations on a Korean Folk Song" by John Barnes Chance (New York: Boosey & Hawkes/Alfred Publishing Company); *English Folk Song Suite* by Ralph Vaughan Williams (New York: Boosey & Hawkes); or "Russian Sailors' Dance," from *The Red Poppy,* by Reinhold Glière, arr. James Curnow (Milwaukee: Hal Leonard Corporation)

- Sequencing MIDI software files of selected world music piece

- Sequencing software such as *Musicshop* (Nashville: Opcode Systems)

## Procedures

1. Ask students to listen to the MIDI file of the selected piece. Explain that they will be performing one part using the controller with an ethnic instrument sound.

2. Tell students to use the printouts of their parts and practice their parts with the MIDI file. Explain that they should focus on expression and technical accuracy.

3. Have students mute their parts on the MIDI file and record their versions onto a new track. Explain that they should perform their parts using an ethnic instrument sound—such as pan flute, shakuhachi, shamisen, koto, kalimba, bagpipe, or shanai—that fits with the culture of the music.

4. Play back the performances and have students assess each other's performances for expression and technical accuracy.

## Indicators of Success

- Students perform their parts with expression and technical accuracy.

*(continued)*

- Parts for selected literature printed in concert key from a notation software program (converted from sequencing MIDI files)

- Printouts of parts from the score, created in MIDI program

## Prior Knowledge and Experiences

- Students have experience playing wind, percussion, or string controllers.

- Students have been rehearsing the selected work.

- Students have listened to recordings of music of diverse genres and cultures.

- Students know the names of ethnic instruments used in General MIDI sounds, such as kalimba.

## Follow-up

- Have some students perform with the group on MIDI controllers using ethnic instrument sounds.

# STANDARD 2D

*Performing on instruments, alone and with others, a varied repertoire of music:* Students perform with expression and technical accuracy a large and varied repertoire of instrumental literature with a level of difficulty of 5, on a scale of 1 to 6.

## Objective

- Students will perform an accompanied level 5 piece with expression and technical accuracy.

## Materials

- Computers connected to powered speakers or headphones
- *Smart Music* (Eden Prairie, MN: Coda Music Technology) accompaniment software and microphone (footswitch optional)
- *Smart Music* software file for Charlie Parker's "Donna Lee"; or another level 5 piece
- Recording of Charlie Parker's "Donna Lee," on *Yardbird Suite—Ultimate Charlie Parker Collection* (WEA/Atlantic/Rhino 72260)
- Printed music for the melody of "Donna Lee," transposed for instruments in the ensemble
- Audiocassette recorder, microphone, and blank tape
- Audio-playback equipment
- Self-evaluation forms with criteria for technical accuracy and expression

## Prior Knowledge and Experiences

- Students have played level 5 music.
- Students have studied various jazz styles and have experience with jazz phrasing.
- Student have experience using *Smart Music*.

## Procedures

1. Have students listen to the Charlie Parker recording of "Donna Lee" for correct style.
2. Tell students to load "Donna Lee" *Smart Music* software file on their workstations and position the microphone.
3. Ask students to practice "Donna Lee" melody, focusing on technical accuracy and expression, along with *Smart Music* until they feel competent to perform for the class.
4. Invite students to perform "Donna Lee" individually for the class. Have students use the self-evaluation form to evaluate their own performances in terms of technical accuracy and expression. Record the performances on cassette tape.

## Indicators of Success

- Students perform on their instruments with technical accuracy and expression.
- Students play the piece in the style they hear on the Charlie Parker recording.

## Follow-up

- Have students improvise on chord changes of "Donna Lee" with *Smart Music* accompaniment.

# STANDARD 3C

***Improvising melodies, variations, and accompaniments:*** *Students improvise original melodies over given chord progressions, each in a consistent style, meter, and tonality.*

## Objective

- Students will improvise melodies over a standard blues progression, singing or performing on instruments.

## Materials

- Computers with General MIDI sound generation (internal sound card—Windows; QuickTime Musical Instruments—Macintosh) connected to powered speakers or headphones; or computers connected to General MIDI keyboards with powered speakers or headphones

- Sequencing software such as *Musicshop* (Nashville: Opcode Systems) or *Cakewalk Home Studio* (Cambridge, MA: Cakewalk)

- Teacher-generated sequencing file of a blues progression to serve as an accompaniment [*Note:* File should be on a loop to enable all students to have the opportunity to improvise.]

- Copies of handout with the traditional blues progression and the blues scale

- Audiocassette recorder, microphone, and blank tapes

- Copies of rubric for student self-assessment (see step 4)

## Procedures

1. Review and practice the blues chord progression and the blues scale. Distribute copies of the rubric for self-assessment.

2. Ask students to improvise a melody over the blues progression.

3. Have students independently work with the blues progression sequence and record their blues improvisations to cassette tape with the blues sequencing file.

4. Direct students to use the rubric for self-assessment for evaluating their improvisations in terms of how well they stayed within tonal and stylistic parameters, as well as how well they maintained the meter.

5. Have each student select his or her improvisation that best meets the rubric descriptors and submit that improvisation for teacher assessment.

## Indicators of Success

- Students improvise melodies over the blues progression.

- Students stay within given tonal and stylistic parameters and maintain the meter in their improvisations.

## Prior Knowledge and Experiences

- Students know how to use sequencing software.
- Students have listened to blues recordings by artists such as Mary Lou Williams, Duke Ellington, and Oscar Peterson.
- Students have worked with the blues progression and the blues scale.

## Follow-up

- Have students transcribe their selected improvisations from the Procedures and enter them into a notation program with blues accompaniment. Then ask students to create a blues melody and insert it after the statement of the improvised melody in order to create a composition that includes their own improvised solo.

# STANDARD 3C

***Improvising melodies, variations, and accompaniments:*** *Students improvise original melodies over given chord progressions, each in a consistent style, meter, and tonality.*

## Objective

- Students will improvise solos over chord changes for pieces they are studying in jazz band, combo, or choir.

## Materials

- Computers with General MIDI sound generation (internal sound card—Windows; QuickTime Musical Instruments—Macintosh) connected to powered speakers or headphones; or computers connected to General MIDI keyboards with powered speakers or headphones

- *Band-in-a-Box* (Victoria, BC: PG Music) accompaniment software

- Ensemble music with chord changes in concert key

- Audiocassette recorder, microphone, and blank tapes

## Prior Knowledge and Experiences

- Students have been rehearsing a selected tune in their jazz group.

- Students have improvised solos over given chord changes.

- Students have experience using *Band-in-a-Box* software.

## Procedures

1. Have students enter the chord changes for the solo they are to improvise in *Band-in-a-Box.*

2. Ask students to assign a style that most closely resembles the written rhythm section style.

3. Ask students to record several versions of the solo section to cassette tape at different tempos and with at least four repeated choruses.

4. Encourage students to use the cassette tape to practice improvising over the solo section. Explain that they should work on eventually being able to play or sing at the correct tempo.

5. Have students play or sing improvised solos with the school jazz group.

## Indicators of Success

- Students improvise melodies over the given chord changes, playing or singing with expression.

- Students improvise melodies in a consistent style, meter, and tonality.

## Follow-up

- Have students use *Smart Music* software (Eden Prairie, MN: Coda Music Technology) to practice improvising melodies in various styles and keys and at various tempos.

# STANDARD 3E

***Improvising melodies, variations, and accompaniments:*** *Students improvise original melodies in a variety of styles, over given chord progressions, each in a consistent style, meter, and tonality.*

## Objective

- Students will improvise solos in two contrasting styles, incorporating elements of the styles of well-known jazz musicians into their solos.

## Materials

- Computers with General MIDI sound generation (internal sound card—Windows; QuickTime Musical Instruments—Macintosh) connected to powered speakers or headphones; or computers connected to General MIDI keyboards with powered speakers or headphones

- *Band-in-a-Box* accompaniment software (Victoria, BC: PG Music)

- Recordings of well-known jazz soloists (see steps 1 and 4)

- *Band-in-a-Box* file and printout of lead sheet for a standard jazz tune

- Audiocassette recorder, microphone, and blank tapes

## Prior Knowledge and Experiences

- Students have experience using *Band-in-a-Box* software.

- Students have created their own *Band-in-a-Box* file of a standard song (or they use a standard song that comes with *Band-in-a-Box* ).

- Students have printed out a lead sheet for a standard song (or they use an already-printed lead sheet).

## Procedures

1. Have students listen to the *Band-in-a-Box* file for the selected standard song and view the chord changes. Then have them click on the "solo" button and view a list of soloists from which they can create computer-generated improvised solos.

2. Ask each student to choose two soloists (preferably musicians who play the same instrument).

3. Direct students to generate solos in the style of one of the soloists and listen to the playback of the computer-generated solo. Tell them to continue to create solos, which will be different every time, until they find the one they like best.

4. Ask students to practice with the computer-generated solo as it plays, or have them print out the solo and practice it independently, isolating devices or techniques that make that musician's style unique. Tell students to make note of these devices or techniques. Then have them listen to recordings of the actual musician and include on their lists any additional devices or techniques the soloist uses.

5. Have students repeat steps 3 and 4 for the second soloist.

6. Ask students to play the standard song without the computer-generated solos. This time have them record themselves playing the melody and improvising at least one chorus of solo in each of the two different styles.

7. Have students turn in a cassette recording of their best improvisation for final assessment.

## Indicators of Success

- Students improvise melodies in two contrasting styles.

- Students incorporate stylistic devices or techniques of two well-known jazz musicians into their improvisations.

## Follow-up

- Have students transcribe solos from recordings of soloists and study their style by playing or singing the transcribed solos.

- Ask students to study other musicians' styles, using the *Band-in-a-Box* computer-generated solo feature.

# STANDARD 4A

***Composing and arranging music within specified guidelines:*** *Students compose music in several distinct styles, demonstrating creativity in using the elements of music for expressive effect.*

## Objective

- Students will compose a short instrumental duet, basing the melody and harmony on a Korean folk-song style.

## Materials

- Computers with General MIDI sound generation (internal sound card—Windows; QuickTime Musical Instruments—Macintosh) connected to powered speakers or head-phones; or computers con-nected to General MIDI key-boards with powered speakers or headphones

- Notation software such as *Encore* (Philadelphia: GVOX), *Finale* (Eden Prairie, MN: Coda Music Technology), or *Overture* (Cambridge, MA: Cakewalk)

- Score and parts for "Variations on a Korean Folk Song," for concert band, by John Barnes Chance (New York: Boosey & Hawkes/Alfred Publishing Company), Level 4

- Copies of teacher-generated worksheet showing one of the pentatonic scales used in "Variations on a Korean Folk Song" in both treble and bass clefs

## Procedures

1. Explain to students that they will be applying their understanding of pentatonic scales and musical expression by composing a short composition for two band instruments. Tell them that pentatonic scales and the expressiveness of "Variations on a Korean Folk Song" will be the inspiration for this composition.

2. Distribute the worksheet and review the concept of pentatonic scales. Have students play excerpts of "Variations on a Korean Folk Song" in which the sound of the pentatonic scale is clearly heard. Discuss the character of the expressiveness in these excerpts. Ask, "When is the music smooth and lyrical and when is it lively and energetic?" "When is it melancholy and when is it dramatic?" Discuss how the composer used the elements of music to achieve these expressive qualities.

3. With notation software, have students decide which band instru-ments, key, and meter signature they will use. Then have them set up a two-staff score for this duet. Encourage them to select an over-all character or mood that they would like to achieve with the melody and to think about the features of the melody that will help convey this character. For example, will they use mostly short or long notes, use simple or complex rhythms, use few or many rests, move mostly by steps or leaps, or use short or long phrases?

4. Give students time to compose a short melody with the notation software, using appropriate pitches and rhythms for the tonality and meter signature. Check the compositions for accuracy in pitch-es and rhythm. Help students use rhythmic and melodic patterns that convey the expressiveness they desire. Suggest that they use dynamics, accents, and articulations that bring out the expressive-ness of the melody.

5. Listen to the completed melodies and discuss possible revisions or additions.

6. Have students revise their melodies, then add a harmonizing part to them. Discuss and demonstrate the use of ostinato, countermelody, and chord roots as possible approaches to adding harmony. Encourage them to select pitches, rhythms, and expression mark-ings that reinforce the expressiveness of the melody.

## Prior Knowledge and Experiences

- Students have rehearsed "Variations on a Korean Folk Song."

- Students can write pentatonic scales and rhythms in a variety of meter signatures.

- Students have basic skills with a notation program.

7. Have students perform their duets on instruments and discuss the strengths and weaknesses. Help students analyze and describe how the elements of their melody and harmony reinforced or detracted from the expressiveness they were trying to achieve.

## Indicators of Success

- Students compose an expressive duet with melody and harmony using pentatonic scales and rhythms.

## Follow-up

- Have students compose a new variation to the Korean folk song used in "Variations on a Korean Folk Song."

# STANDARD 4B

*Composing and arranging music within specified guidelines:* Students arrange pieces for voices
or instruments other than those for which the pieces were written in ways that preserve or
enhance the expressive effect of the music.

## Objective

- Students will arrange an instrumental music passage for an SATB choral ensemble.

## Materials

- Computers with General MIDI sound generation (internal sound card—Windows; QuickTime Musical Instruments—Macintosh) connected to powered speakers or headphones; or computers connected to General MIDI keyboards with powered speakers or headphones

- Notation software such as *Encore* (Philadelphia: GVOX), *Finale* (Eden Prairie, MN: Coda Music Technology), or *Overture* (Cambridge, MA: Cakewalk)

- Teacher-generated notation software file of eight measures or more of J. S. Bach's "Orchestral Suite no. 3 in D (BWV. 1068), Air" [*Note:* MIDI files for this piece can be downloaded from Classical Archives, http://www.prs.net.]

- Recording of "J. S. Bach: Air," from *Hush,* performed by Yo-Yo Ma and Bobby McFerrin (Sony CD SK48177); and recording of an instrumental version of this piece

## Procedures

1. Explain to students that arrangers of choral music have often been inspired by instrumental music and have rearranged it for voices, achieving a new expressive effect compared to the original instrumental version. Ask students if they can name any vocal groups that have sung instrumental music.

2. Play the recording of Take 6, Swingle Singers, or another vocal group that sings instrumental music. Play the recording of "J. S. Bach: Air" by Yo-Yo Ma and Bobby McFerrin and an instrumental version of this piece. Discuss the differences in expressive quality and the music elements that contribute to this quality.

3. Explain to students that they will arrange a short passage from the original instrumental version of "Air" (see "Air—Original for Strings" on page 118) for SATB voices as a way to understand the unique challenges of rearranging and performing instrumental music for voices. Review the comfortable singing ranges for soprano, alto, tenor, and baritone voices.

4. Using the notation file of eight measures or more of "Air," guide students in some of the changes they will need to make so that each part is singable (see "Air—Rearranged for Voices" on page 118). For example, the key needs to be changed so that it is within range of the sopranos, octaves may need to be changed for individual notes, or rapid sixteenth-note rhythms may need to be simplified to eighth-note rhythms.

5. Give students ample time to make the changes needed in at least eight measures, encouraging them to listen often and try singing parts on neutral syllables as they make the changes.

6. When students have finished, have them compare their arrangements and point out different solutions to musical problems.

7. Select a few arrangements to rehearse and perform with the choral ensemble.

- Recordings of vocal ensembles performing instrumental pieces rearranged for voice, such as "A Quiet Place" by Take 6, on *Take 6 Greatest Hits* (Warner 47375); or "English Suite no. 2, Bourrée I," on *Jazz Sebastien Bach,* performed by the Swingle Singers (Philips 824 703-2)

## Prior Knowledge and Experiences

- Students have experience using basic features of notation software, such as entering notes, changing pitches, and changing key signatures.

- Student have experience singing in SATB ensembles.

## Indicators of Success

- Students rearrange at least eight measures of "Air" for voices, using correct singing ranges for each voice and making changes needed for each part to be more singable.

## Follow-up

- Select other pieces from the recordings by the Swingle Singers and by Yo-Yo Ma and Bobby McFerrin. Have students watch the instrumental scores as they listen to these pieces. Then have them try rearranging one or more of the pieces.

*(continued)*

**Air—Original for Strings**

**Air—Rearranged for Voices**

*Choral*

*Proficient*

**Reading and notating music:** *Students sightread, accurately and expressively, music with a level of difficulty of 3, on a scale of 1 to 6.*

## Objective

- Students will accurately and expressively sightread selected portions of their voice parts in a level 3 choral work, along with accompaniment or other voice parts.

## Materials

- Computers with General MIDI sound generation (internal sound card—Windows; QuickTime Musical Instruments—Macintosh) connected to powered speakers or headphones; or computers connected to General MIDI keyboards with powered speakers or headphones

- Notation software such as *Finale* (Eden Prairie, MN: Coda Music Technology) or *Encore* (Philadelphia: GVOX)

- Teacher-prepared notation file of selected portions of "For the Beauty of the Earth" by John Rutter (Chapel Hill, NC: Hinshaw Music); or another level 3 SATB choral work

- Audiocassette recorder, microphone, and blank tapes

## Prior Knowledge and Experiences

- Students can sightread their voice parts in level 2 SATB music.

- Students have experience using notation files, including opening and closing, muting and unmuting staves for playback, and starting to play at a designated measure.

## Procedures

1. Assign students selected measures of "For the Beauty of the Earth" for sightreading.

2. Have students, working alone in a practice room or other isolated space, open the notation file of "For the Beauty of the Earth." Tell them to mute all of the staves for voice parts so that they hear only the accompaniment.

3. Have students play the designated measures of the score and sightread their voice parts for the selected measures. Tell them to repeat the sightreading for a designated number of times.

4. Direct students to unmute the staff with their own voice part and sing the part as it is played back by the notation program in order to check their accuracy.

5. Have students unmute the staves for the voice parts other than their own and sing their part along with the other parts being played by the notation program.

6. As an assessment, have students record themselves singing their parts either with the accompaniment only or with the accompaniment and other voice parts, according to your assignment.

## Indicators of Success

- Students accurately sightread their individual voice parts with accompaniment or with other voice parts played back by a notation program.

## Follow-up

- Have students sightread their individual voice parts with only one other voice part and no accompaniment.

- Have students sightread other pieces with a difficulty level of 3 in a variety of styles.

# STANDARD 7B

***Evaluating music and music performances:*** *Students evaluate a performance, composition, arrangement, or improvisation by comparing it to similar or exemplary models.*

## Objective

- Students will critically evaluate music rehearsals of their ensemble, identify important compositional aspects and characteristics of the compositions, and compare their performances.

## Materials

- Computers with Internet access

- Software for sending and receiving e-mail, such as web browsers *Internet Explorer* (Redmond, WA: Microsoft Corporation) or *Netscape Navigator* (Mountain View, CA: Netscape)

- E-mail mailing list (listserv) for your ensemble [*Note:* Services for mailing lists are available free from companies such as Yahoo Groups (http://www.yahoo.com).]

- VCR with headphones

- Teacher-generated rehearsal critique form (see Sample Rehearsal Critique Form)

- Video recording of a well-done rehearsal (Video A), teacher-critiqued using the rehearsal critique form (Critique A)

- Video recording of an average rehearsal (Video B)

## Prior Knowledge and Experiences

- Students have experience using e-mail.

- Students have experience analyzing and describing music performances.

## Procedures

1. Assign five to seven students to each view Video A and read your Critique A. Then, have each of these students critique Video B, using the rehearsal critique form, by comparing Video A and Critique A to Video B. Have students e-mail their responses (Critique B) to the ensemble mailing list within a week.

2. Compare the students' responses (Critique B) to your own critique, and, using the mailing list, respond to the students' critiques with suggestions and questions. Ask all members of the ensemble to read the students' critiques and your reactions to them by using the archiving feature of the mailing list, where all messages are stored for re-reading.

3. From the critiques, compile students' comments relating to challenges, interesting features, and important aspects of the composition and its performance. Send this compilation to the ensemble mailing list and ask all students to read it.

4. For each student critique (Critique B), ask all students to re-read the archived messages and select the three or four comments that best represent their experiences and thoughts.

5. Use the most appropriate of the selected comments for program notes in upcoming concert programs. Repeat this cycle with a new group of five to seven students as often as desired.

## Indicators of Success

- Students make appropriate comments about their ensemble rehearsals, pointing out areas that need further attention and areas of success.

- Students describe how their performance (individual and as a section) fits into the context of the whole composition.

## Follow-up

- Videotape individual sections of the ensemble and apply the process used in the Procedures.

- Have students evaluate videotaped performances (past and present) by their ensemble.

- Have students videotape and critique themselves in solo and small-ensemble settings.

# Sample Rehearsal Critique Form

How well did we: (circle your rating)

- follow conducting gestures          Poorly 1  2  3  4  5 Very Well

- sing/play with good tone          Poorly 1  2  3  4  5 Very Well

- sing/play as an ensemble          Poorly 1  2  3  4  5 Very Well

- important elements, like melody and

    dynamics, are heard and appropriate     Poorly 1  2  3  4  5 Very Well

- bring out solo lines in the music      Poorly 1  2  3  4  5 Very Well

- start and end phrases/sections together    Poorly 1  2  3  4  5 Very Well

Composition Evaluation: _____ (composition to be assigned by teacher)

1. What part or section of the composition seems to need the most work? What aspects (i.e., correct notes, rhythmic accuracy, balance, articulation, etc.) need attention in this section? What specific strategies do you think we need to use to improve this?

2. If you were to describe this composition to someone who had never heard it, what would you tell them?

3. What section of the composition do you think is the most effective musically? Why? Which structural elements (such as melody, articulation, texture) help make this section so effective? What strategies would you suggest so that we could make the rest of the composition as effective as this section?

4. What musical aspects of this composition were the most difficult to master for you as a performer? If we could start practicing this composition again from the first rehearsal, what strategies could we have used to make it easier to work on?

5. What did you learn about this composition from listening and watching the rehearsal that you didn't know before?

6. What do you feel your section needs to do better in this composition to make our performances better? What do you personally need to do?

7. Discuss the role your section played in the various sections of this composition (e.g., chordal accompaniment, melody, countermelody, rhythmic interest). Discuss your contribution in the various sections of this composition.

# STANDARD 8C

***Understanding relationships between music, the other arts, and disciplines outside the arts:*** *Students explain ways in which the principles and subject matter of various disciplines outside the arts are interrelated with those of music.*

## Objective

- Students will use digital effects to develop a vocal soundscape based upon a poem or short essay they have written and describe how their vocal settings convey images or feelings.

## Materials

- Four-track recorder
- Microphone
- Sound effects processor
- Poems or short essays from English class
- Copies of rubric for self-evaluation

## Prior Knowledge and Experiences

- Students have rehearsed and performed speech compositions.

## Other Requirements

- Arrangement with English teacher to have students play their compositions for combined music and English classes (see step 4)

## Procedures

1. Assign small groups of students to record expressive readings of a poem or essay on a four-track recorder.

2. Instruct students to use the sound effects processor, rhythmic chanting, and other vocal expressions to record background tracks for their reading and create a vocal soundscape.

3. Ask students to review their recordings and re-record as needed to adjust the tracks' volume, pan, and so on.

4. Have students play their recordings for combined music and English classes. Tell students to evaluate the effectiveness of the compositions using the given rubric. Ask them to explain how the music conveys images or feelings from their readings.

## Indicators of Success

- Students create effective vocal settings of poems and essays.
- Students describe how their vocal settings convey images or feelings from their readings.

## Follow-up

- Have students record their compositions to CD.

# STANDARD 9A

***Understanding music in relation to history and culture:*** *Students classify by genre or style and by historical period or culture unfamiliar but representative aural examples of music and explain the reasoning behind their classifications.*

## Objective

■ Students will develop a portfolio of materials related to John Philip Sousa and the march genre, classify marches by genre and historical period, and explain the reasoning for their classifications.

## Materials

■ Computers that have Internet access

■ Web browser software such as *Netscape Communicator* (Mountain View, CA: Netscape) or *Internet Explorer* (Redmond, WA: Microsoft Corporation)

■ Teacher-prepared Webquest on John Philip Sousa (http://edweb.sdsu.edu/webquest/LessonTemplate.html) (see page 124)

■ Teacher-prepared rubric (http://edweb.sdsu.edu/triton/July/rubrics/Rubrics_for_Web_Lessons.html)

■ Score and parts for a march by John Philip Sousa

## Prior Knowledge and Experiences

■ Students have experience browsing the Internet.

■ Students have been rehearsing the selected march by John Philip Sousa.

## Procedures

1. Have students, working individually or in small groups, read and follow the instructions on the John Philip Sousa WebQuest. [*Note:* Students might be excused from rehearsal a few at a time, do the work at home, or view the links together as a class.] Distribute the rubric you have prepared.

2. Assign students to assemble a portfolio on John Philip Sousa, including a newspaper article they write, a march discussion, a journal, and other information. [*Note:* Depending upon the design, projects may take as long as four weeks to complete.]

3. Assess projects according to the rubric.

4. Have students listen to marches by Sousa and other composers that are unfamiliar to them, as well as to works from other genres and historical periods that they have studied. Ask them to classify these works by genre and by historical period and to explain the reasoning for their classifications.

5. Continue rehearsal of the selected march by John Philip Sousa. In the course of the rehearsal, ask students questions about Sousa, the march form, and the era of the Sousa band.

## Indicators of Success

■ Students describe Sousa's life, identify major soloists with the Sousa band, list and describe Sousa marches, discuss the concerts and tours of the Sousa band, and discuss the lifestyle of that era.

■ Students respond to verbal questions from the teacher about Sousa, the march form, and the era of the Sousa band during the course of rehearsal.

■ Students classify other aural examples of marches, as well as works of other genres that they have studied, according to genre and historical period and explain the reasoning for their classifications.

## Follow-up

■ Display samples from the portfolios created by students in the Procedures at the concert where the Sousa march is performed.

*(continued)*

# WebQuest on John Philip Sousa

A. Introduction: John Philip Sousa, the "March King," was a major influence on the development of bands in the United States. This WebQuest will provide you with further insight into Sousa, his music, and the time period in which he lived. This information will enable you to better understand and perform the music of Sousa that we are studying in band.

B. Task: By the completion of this lesson, you will be able to describe the life of John Philip Sousa, identify major soloists with the Sousa band, list and describe marches composed by John Philip Sousa, discuss the concerts and tours of the Sousa band, and discuss the lifestyle of that era.

C. Process:

(1) You are a reporter from the newspaper of a small town where the Sousa band will perform a concert. You have been fortunate enough to secure an interview with Mr. Sousa. Write the article that will appear in the newspaper following the interview. This article should include biographical information on Mr. Sousa and background material on the Sousa band.

(2) Listen to examples (MIDI files) of at least six different marches by Sousa; list them and the dates they were composed. Describe how these marches are similar. Describe how they are different. Which one is your favorite? Why?

(3) You are a member of the Sousa band. You keep a journal describing your life while on tour with the band. Write a journal entry discussing a typical day in your life. Include a discussion of both the musical parts of your life (how many concerts per day you play, what those concerts are like, some of the soloists featured with the band, etc.), but also the nonmusical parts of your life (how you travel, what you do for fun, names of some of your friends in the band, popular entertainers, sports figures, writers, etc.). These are just some ideas to get you started. You may write about these or other things in your journal.

D. Resources:

John Philip Sousa (http://www.dws.org/sousa)

The Music of John Philip Sousa (http://www.dws.org/sousa/music.htm)

Sousa Archives for Band Research (http://www.library.uiuc.edu/sousa)

The United States Marine Band—John Philip Sousa (http://www.marineband.usmc.mil/edu_sousa.html)

HyperHistory (http://www.hyperhistory.com/online_n2/History_n2/a.html)

Britannica.com (http://www.britannica.com)

E. Evaluation:

Assemble a portfolio of your WebQuest, including your newspaper article, march discussion, journal, and any other information you desire.

F. Conclusion:

John Philip Sousa has had a lasting influence on bands and band music. Because you are a band musician, Sousa is part of your heritage.

# THEORY, MUSIC TECHNOLOGY, KEYBOARDS, MUSIC HISTORY
## Grades 9–12

# STANDARD 1B

*Proficient*

***Singing, alone and with others, a varied repertoire of music:*** *Students sing music written in four parts, with and without accompaniment.*

## Objective

- Students will create three upper voices over a given bass part for a four-part chorale and sing the resulting chorale.

## Materials

- Computers with General MIDI sound generation (internal sound card—Windows; QuickTime Musical Instruments—Macintosh) connected to powered speakers or headphones; or computers connected to General MIDI keyboards with powered speakers or headphones

- Notation software such as *Music Time* (Philadelphia: GVOX) or *Print Music* (Eden Prairie, MN: Coda Music Technology)

- Computer display projector and screen

- Teacher-generated notation file of eight measures with three empty staves (soprano, alto, tenor), bass staff with bass notated, and chord symbols above the score

## Prior Knowledge and Experiences

- Students can name chord tones and sing pitches in diatonic chords.

- Students have experience singing four-part chorales.

## Procedures

1. Using the notation software and projector, display and play the notation file.

2. Work through the file with students, having them notate soprano, alto, and tenor parts above the given bass part and discuss voice leading.

3. Play back each voice separately, having students sing along and raise their hands at any points at which the voice leading is not comfortable to them.

4. Have students correct their note choices and repeat step 3 until they are satisfied with the voice leading.

5. Have students sing all four parts with and without accompaniment.

## Indicators of Success

- Students listen for effective voice leading and make appropriate decisions in writing parts for a four-part chorale.

- Students sing the completed chorale with and without accompaniment.

## Follow-up

- Have small groups of students complete a four-part voice leading exercise on their own.

# STANDARD 1C

***Singing, alone and with others, a varied repertoire of music:*** *Students demonstrate well-developed ensemble skills.*

## Objective

- Students will sing improvised solo ("call") and harmonized back-up vocals ("responses") in a twelve-bar blues, demonstrating well-developed ensemble skills.

## Materials

- Computers with microphones, connected to General MIDI keyboards, with powered speakers or headphones

- Sequencing software with digital audio such as *Cakewalk Home Studio* (Cambridge, MA: Cakewalk), *Metro 5* (Cambridge, MA: Cakewalk), or *MicroLogic* (Grass Valley, CA: Emagic Soft- und Hardware GmbH/Emagic, Inc.)

- Accompaniment software such as *Band-in-a-Box* (Victoria, BC: PG Music) or *Visual Arranger* (Buena Vista, CA: Yamaha Corporation of America)

## Prior Knowledge and Experiences

- Students have generated a software MIDI file of a twelve-bar blues using accompaniment software.

## Procedures

1. Ask students to import their MIDI file of a twelve-bar blues accompaniment into the sequencing software program with digital audio.

2. Discuss ensemble singing skills, including blend, balance, phrasing, and articulation.

3. Model, then have students improvise and record, onto the digital audio tracks of the sequencing file, a solo ("call") and harmonized back-up vocal parts ("response") over the blues accompaniment using keyboard and software. Remind students to incorporate the ensemble skills they discussed.

4. Have students record themselves singing an improvised solo onto a digital audio track of the sequence.

5. Assign groups of students to improvise and then rehearse singing the back-up vocals (like back-up singers) and record their performance onto another digital audio track.

6. Play back the performances and have students discuss how well each group sang as an ensemble.

## Indicators of Success

- Students improvise solos and back-up vocal parts over a twelve-bar blues accompaniment.

- Students improvise parts that complement the underlying harmony.

- Students demonstrate well-developed ensemble skills.

## Follow-up

- Have students resave their MIDI/audio files in the WAV format. Then use a CD burner to store the performances on compact disc.

# STANDARD 2B

*Proficient*

***Performing on instruments, alone and with others, a varied repertoire of music:*** *Students perform an appropriate part in an ensemble, demonstrating well-developed ensemble skills.*

## Objective

■ Students will perform keyboard or synthesizer parts, using traditional and nontraditional sounds and blending and balancing with other parts.

## Materials

■ Electronic keyboards or synthesizers, set up for individuals or pairs

■ Printed score (for each workstation) with at least four different parts, with a level of difficulty of 3 or higher

■ Audiocassette recorder, microphone, and blank tapes

## Prior Knowledge and Experiences

■ Students have experience playing electronic keyboards or synthesizers and are familiar with the available sounds.

■ Students can read music from a score.

## Procedures

1. Assign students at each workstation a part from the score. Have students decide which sound best simulates the instrument for which the part was written. Tell them to begin to think of a nontraditional part to be used later.

2. Check each station to listen to the sound students have chosen, as well as to how well students are progressing in playing their parts.

3. Have students play their parts individually for the class. Tell other students to play their parts with the external sound turned off so that only the solo parts are heard for now.

4. Have all students play their parts as an ensemble, together with the traditional instrument sounds. Lead students in a discussion about balance and blend, having them describe how well the selected instrument sounds work. Record the performance.

5. Ask all students to play their parts again, this time with nontraditional sounds for their parts. Again, have students describe whether the selected instruments balance and blend well with each other. Record the performance.

6. Play back the recordings with traditional and nontraditional sounds and have students compare them, focusing on balance and blend. Ask them to evaluate the effectiveness of the traditional versus the nontraditional sounds.

## Indicators of Success

■ Students play keyboard or synthesizer parts, using traditional and nontraditional sounds.

■ Students make instrument selections that enable them to blend and balance their parts well with each other.

## Follow-up

■ Have students record all parts from the score into a sequencer or notation program. Assign traditional and nontraditional sounds to each part.

# STANDARD 2C

*Proficient*

**Performing on instruments, alone and with others, a varied repertoire of music:** *Students perform in small ensembles with one student on a part.*

## Objective

- Students will perform a four-part Bach chorale with one person on each part.

## Materials

- Electronic keyboards or synthesizers, set up for individuals or pairs
- Computer with General MIDI sound generation (internal sound card—Windows; QuickTime Musical Instruments—Macintosh) connected to powered speakers or headphones
- Sequencing or notation software for playback of MIDI file; or keyboards with disk drives that can open and play MIDI files
- Copy of J. S. Bach's "Break Forth, O Beauteous Heavenly Light," or another Bach chorale, for each workstation
- *Bach Chorale Standard MIDI Files* (Pacific, MO: Mel Bay), IBM (95050IMD); Macintosh (95050MMD)
- Audiocassette recorder, microphone, and blank tape

## Procedures

1. Have students listen to MIDI files of Bach chorales, focusing on how well the four parts work together.

2. Lead a discussion on Bach-chorale style. Ask students to illustrate their comments by playing back MIDI files of chorales at appropriate points.

3. Assign each student to one of the four parts of the chorale "Break Forth, O Beauteous Heavenly Light."

4. Ask students to find a sound on the keyboard or synthesizer that they feel best fits the Baroque style. Have them practice their parts of the chorale. Monitor the students' work, checking to make sure that they are using instrument sounds that would be appropriate for the Baroque era.

5. Divide class into groups of four, with one student on each part, and have each group perform the chorale together. When students are listening to another group play, ask them to assess both the individual parts and the blend of voices.

6. After each group performance, have students who were listening give suggestions for improvements or suggest other instrument sounds that could be used to make the chorale sound closer to what a Baroque chorale would sound like.

7. Record each group's performance. Play back the performances and have the groups evaluate themselves on both the accuracy of their performances and the effectiveness of their ensemble skills.

## Indicators of Success

- Students perform the four-part Bach chorale with one person on each part, demonstrating accuracy and good blend of the parts.

## Prior Knowledge and Experiences

- Students have experience playing electronic keyboards or synthesizers.
- Students can read music from a score.
- Students have experience using the selected sequencing or notation software.
- Students can identify the sounds of instruments used during the Baroque era.

## Follow-up

- Have students compare the recordings from the Procedures to the original MIDI files and to professional recordings of "Break Forth, O Beauteous Heavenly Light."

# STANDARD 3A

**Improvising melodies, variations, and accompaniments:** *Students improvise stylistically appropriate harmonizing parts.*

## Objective

- Students will improvise and record one harmonizing horn part (clarinet or trombone sound) and one rhythm section (chords or bass) part in the New Orleans jazz style.

## Materials

- Computers connected to General MIDI keyboards with powered speakers or headphones

- Sequencing software such as *Musicshop* (Nashville: Opcode Systems) or *Cakewalk Home Studio* (Cambridge, MA: Cakewalk)

- Teacher-prepared sequencing file of "When the Saints Go Marchin' In" (with melody and drums only)

- Lead sheets for "When the Saints Go Marchin' In"

## Prior Knowledge and Experiences

- Students can use basic chord symbols.

- Students can play the melody, chords, and bass line to "When the Saints Go Marchin' In."

## Procedures

1. Distribute lead sheets and have students perform the chord progression for "When the Saints Go Marchin' In" at the keyboard.

2. Review the concept of guide tones and how they are used. Have students learn to locate guide tones in "Saints" and play them as whole notes.

3. Demonstrate rhythmic, then melodic, embellishment of the "Saints" melody.

4. Have students practice rhythmic embellishments to the guide-tone line. Then have students practice melodic embellishments, using diatonic upper and lower neighbors.

5. Tell students to practice applying the same techniques (rhythmic and melodic embellishment) to the bass line. Then have them apply rhythmic embellishment to the chords.

6. Have students, working independently or in groups at their workstations, open the prepared "Saints" sequencing file. Ask each student to choose either clarinet or trombone, set up a track with that instrument assigned, and record an improvised harmony line based on a guide-tone line for the chords on the lead sheet for "Saints."

7. Ask each student to choose either chords (piano or banjo) or bass. Then have each student set up a track to record either the chord progression or the bass line with appropriate embellishment. Tell students to save their work to disk.

## Indicators of Success

- Students demonstrate their understanding of improvisational techniques (rhythmic and melodic embellishment) and harmonically correct guide-tone lines.

- Students demonstrate their understanding of instrument functions in the New Orleans style.

- Students have experience with the concept of "guide tones" (the third and the seventh of all chords in a succession of chords) as a means of creating a harmony line [*Note:* See Blues Lines Using Guide Tones (http://www.music.sc.edu/ Departments/Jazz/ BluesGT.pdf).]

- Students have listened to New Orleans-style music (such as Louis Armstrong, Jelly Roll Morton, or Preservation Hall) and to uses of specific instruments within the style.

- Students have experience using the selected sequencing software for recording and editing.

## Follow-up

- Give students a lead sheet for a different song, along with a prepared accompaniment file. Have them determine their own guide-tone lines and use them as the basis for improvisations.

# STANDARD 4B

*Proficient*

**Composing and arranging music within specified guidelines:** *Students arrange pieces for voices or instruments other than those for which the pieces were written in ways that preserve or enhance the expressive effect of the music.*

## Objective

- Students will arrange a piano or organ piece for an instrumental quartet or quintet.

## Materials

- Computers connected to General MIDI keyboards with powered speakers or head-phones

- Notation software such as *Encore* (Philadelphia: GVOX) or *Finale* (Eden Prairie, MN: Coda Music Technology)

- Recording of *Pictures at an Exhibition*—for piano by Modest Mussorgsky, and for orchestra, arr. Maurice Ravel; or another piano work that has been orchestrated

- Book of Handel keyboard works or Bach chorales

## Prior Knowledge and Experiences

- Students have basic skills with notation software.

- Students have a basic knowledge of instrument ranges and the traditional groupings of instruments into small ensembles.

- Students have selected a keyboard work and identified an instrumental quartet or quintet for which to arrange the work.

## Procedures

1. Guide students in listening and discussing the original and orchestrated versions of *Pictures at an Exhibition*. Speculate on why Ravel may have selected specific instruments for certain passages. Discuss some of the decisions he made.

2. Play the students' selected keyboard works, or have them or other students play the works so that they can hear the style and expressive quality. Briefly discuss the melodic, rhythmic, and harmonic elements and how these might suggest approaches for arranging.

3. Using notation software, guide students in setting up a score for their ensemble arrangement with staves in correct order, clefs, key and meter signatures, and instrument program numbers (patches). Have students determine which instruments will play which lines. Ask them to consider whether instruments should ever switch lines to create a more effective arrangement.

4. Allow sufficient time for students to enter the music using step-time entry and real-time entry. [*Note:* Step-time entry allows the user to enter each pitch with a specific rhythmic duration; (for example, quarter note or eighth note) one step at a time. This is done by clicking notes onto a staff with a mouse or by playing a pitch on a MIDI keyboard after a duration has been specified.] Work individually with each student as needed. Encourage students to make creative decisions, while at the same time retaining the original expressive effect of the music.

5. After students have entered their music, have them play their arrangements for each other. Encourage discussion of what worked well and what did not and about how to improve problem areas.

6. Have students print scores and extract parts. Then, if appropriate student instrumentalists are available, have them perform selected arrangements on band and orchestra instruments.

## Indicators of Success

- Students arrange a keyboard work for instrumental quartet or quintet, preserving the expressive effect of the original piece.

## Follow-up

- Give students a keyboard piece to arrange for a larger group.

# STANDARD 4B

*Proficient*

*Composing and arranging music within specified guidelines: Students arrange pieces for voices or instruments other than those for which the pieces were written in ways that preserve or enhance the expressive effect of the music.*

## Objective

■ Students will arrange musical excerpts, enhancing the expressive effect of the music.

## Materials

■ Computers connected to General MIDI keyboards with powered speakers or headphones

■ Notation software such as *Finale* (Eden Prairie, MN: Coda Music Technology) or *Sibelius* (Cambridge, England: The Sibelius Group), with real-time recording capabilities; or sequencing software with notational capabilities

■ Various musical excerpts prerecorded by teacher using notation or sequencing software (see step 1)

## Prior Knowledge and Experiences

■ Students have used selected notation or sequencing software.

■ Students have experience exploring the many sound capabilities of General MIDI keyboards.

## Procedures

1. Have students open prerecorded files that contain three eight-measure excerpts written for various instruments in various styles. [*Note:* To make the excerpts mechanical, not expressive, there should be no use of tempo changes, dynamics, accents, or articulations, etc.]

2. Instruct students to arrange each excerpt using notation software. Tell them they should use the proper sound of the instrument for which each excerpt is voiced and add tempo changes, dynamics, accents, articulations, and so on, to make each excerpt sound as expressive as possible.

3. Have students use the pitch-bend or modulation wheels to add subtle pitch changes and vibrato. Then, have them use the software to mute one instrument part and practice playing it as the software plays the other instruments parts of the arrangement, adding pitch bend and modulation as they play.

4. Have students record the part they practiced on another MIDI channel for playback.

5. Play back the recordings for the class, having students listen for technical accuracy and for how effectively each student achieved expression by adding tempo changes, dynamics, accents, articulations, and so on, through pitch-bend or modulation wheels.

## Indicators of Success

■ Students arrange given musical excerpts in ways that enhance their expressiveness.

■ Students arrange given musical excerpts with technical accuracy.

## Follow-up

■ Have students record their own compositions or improvisations and arrange them to create expressive MIDI files.

# STANDARD 6A

*Listening to, analyzing, and describing music: Students analyze aural examples of a varied repertoire of music, representing diverse genres and cultures, by describing the uses of elements of music and expressive devices.*

## Objective

■ Students will compare, contrast, and describe the major rhythmic, accompaniment, and instrumentation elements in different styles of music.

## Materials

■ Computers with General MIDI sound generation (internal sound card—Windows; QuickTime Musical Instruments—Macintosh) connected to powered speakers or headphones; or computers connected to General MIDI keyboards with powered speakers or headphones

■ *Band-in-a-Box* (Victoria, BC: PG Music) accompaniment software

## Prior Knowledge and Experiences

■ Students have been studying background information on styles to be demonstrated in the lesson, including jazz swing, a Latin style such as bossa nova, and reggae.

■ Students understand the difference between "even" eighth notes and "swing" eighth notes.

■ Students can identify instruments most commonly used in a particular style of music.

## Procedures

1. From the "Songs" folder in *Band-in-a-Box*, select the song "Jay's Blues."

2. Using the *Band-in-a-Box* software, play the song for the class using the default style (in this case, jazz swing). Discuss with the class the basic characteristics of the style, including the default instrumentation, "swing" eighth notes, and rhythm section styles. [*Note:* Rhythm section styles can be changed within *Band-in-a-Box* under the styles button.]

3. Make changes in the instrumentation by selecting different piano or bass sounds at the top of the screen. Select piano or bass, and then change to different types of pianos or basses. Discuss how different instruments can affect the feel and sound of a song even though the instruments are playing the same notes.

4. Choose a Latin style such as bossa nova, which will change the feel of the eighth notes from "swing" to "even." Discuss how both the influence of the Latin style and the change in eighth notes affect the feel of the song.

5. Choose another style such as reggae, and discuss how the style affects the feel of the song.

6. While still in the reggae style, discuss how tempo can affect the feel of a song. Have students determine which tempo is best for the reggae style.

7. Have students choose other songs and styles. Have them make suggestions for changes in style, including changes in rhythms, tempo, and instrumentation.

## Indicators of Success

■ Students demonstrate their knowledge of musical styles through discussion of characteristics of various styles of music, including the major rhythmic, accompaniment, and instrumentation elements of each style.

## Follow-up

■ Have students work independently at workstations with one song and create several versions of it using different styles, tempos, and instruments. Then have them present their versions to the class, explaining how they changed the original version to new styles.

# STANDARD 6A

*Proficient*

*Listening to, analyzing, and describing music:* Students analyze aural examples of a varied repertoire of music, representing diverse genres and cultures, by describing the uses of elements of music and expressive devices.

## Objective

- Students will analyze and describe compositions representing diverse genres and cultures.

## Materials

- Computers that have Internet access

- Student e-mail accounts

- List of teacher-identified recordings, representing diverse genres or cultures that students listen to online [*Note:* These can be accessed through companies that sell recordings, such as Amazon (http://www.amazon.com) and CD Now (http://www.cdnow.com).]

- Software such as *RealPlayer* (Seattle: RealNetworks) that enables user to hear music recordings from the Internet

- Recording of a short selection or music excerpt (see step 2)

## Prior Knowledge and Experiences

- Students have experience using e-mail and using web sites for listening to recordings.

## Procedures

1. Review with students elements of music and various expressive characteristics of music.

2. As a class, have students listen to a short selection or excerpt of a composition, focusing on the elements of music and the various characteristics of music.

3. Discuss with the class which elements of music are the primary focus and which are the secondary focus in the music on the recording. Also discuss devices the composer used to create interest, including expressive aspects of the music.

4. Distribute the list of selected recordings, along with web addresses for listening to the selections online.

5. Ask students to investigate one selection and to e-mail you within a week with their thoughts describing primary and secondary focuses in the music and devices the composer used to create interest, including expressive elements.

6. Via e-mail, talk with individual students, guiding them as needed to further investigate elements they may have missed or discussed lightly.

7. After several e-mail interactions, compile particularly insightful and interesting comments and, after students have listened to the selection in class, share some of the comments with the class.

## Indicators of Success

- Students identify primary and secondary focuses of selected pieces.

- Student identify composer techniques that create interest, including expressive devices.

## Follow-up

- Create a listserv for the class so that students can talk with each other about different pieces of music.

# STANDARD 6E
*Advanced*

*Listening to, analyzing, and describing music:* Students compare ways in which musical materials are used in a given example relative to ways in which they are used in other works of the same genre or style.

## Objective

■ Students will compare various styles of jazz and describe similarities and differences.

## Materials

■ Computers that have Internet access and a CD- or DVD-ROM player, and that are connected to powered speakers or headphones

■ *The Instrumental History of Jazz* two-CD set, including enhanced CD, written by Willie L. Hill, Jr., compiled by Willie L. Hill, Jr., and Carl Griffin (International Association of Jazz Educators/N2K Encoded Jazz, 1997; available from MENC)

■ Software such as *RealPlayer* (Seattle: RealNetworks) that enables user to hear music recordings from the Internet

■ Teacher-generated bookmarks to the Thelonious Monk Institute of Jazz web site's jazz curriculum, Jazz in America (http://jazzinamerica.com)

## Prior Knowledge and Experiences

■ Students have experience using the Internet to listen to recordings.

## Procedures

1. Lead students in a discussion of the roots of jazz. Include in the discussion how jazz developed in America out of the African-American experience, with its roots going back to Africa and Europe and the music of slavery times (work songs, spirituals, blues, brass band music, and ragtime).

2. Have students view video clips and read short descriptions of different eras of jazz from *The Instrumental History of Jazz* (from the section "Early Jazz" through the section "Mainstream and Beyond").

3. Ask students to listen to recordings from five different eras, using either the Jazz in America web site or *The Instrumental History of Jazz,* and compare styles by identifying similarities and differences. [*Note:* Songs and styles are listed in Jazz Recordings section of Grade 11, Lesson Plan 1 on web site.]

4. Have students identify characteristics of various styles of jazz that are similar (swing feel and syncopation) and elements that are different (use of improvisation, instruments, and harmony).

5. Discuss with students the evolution of jazz as they heard it in the music. [*Note:* They should recognize the use of increasingly complex harmonies and improvisations, better recording quality, and electronic instruments.]

## Indicators of Success

■ Students identify characteristics of various jazz styles that are similar and different.

■ Students identify the ways in which jazz evolved in regard to use of harmonies, improvisation, and instruments.

## Follow-up

■ Have students investigate the topics of improvisation, rhythm, sounds and instruments, and harmony and form on the jazzinamerica web site (Grade 11, Lesson Plan 2).

■ Ask students to compare styles and eras of jazz piano on the CD-ROM *Dick Hyman's Century of Jazz Piano* (West New York, NJ: JSS Music, 1998), including the piano styles boogie-woogie and stride. Have them listen to piano players in various styles of jazz.

# STANDARD 7A

*Evaluating music and music performances: Students evolve specific criteria for making informed, critical evaluations of the quality and effectiveness of performances, compositions, arrangements, and improvisations and apply the criteria in their personal participation in music.*

## Objective

- Students will develop and apply criteria for evaluating a recording of a live performance for its balance, pan, equalization, and effects processing and adjust these in the final mix to enhance the original recording.

## Materials

- Multi-track recording equipment such as a multi-track tape recorder, hard disk recorder with appropriate microphones and mixer, or a digital audio sequencer

- Access to equalization and effects processing (software or hardware)

- Stereo cassette recorder for final mixdown

- Music for performance

## Prior Knowledge and Experiences

- Students have experience operating multi-track recording equipment and using multi-track recording techniques.

- Students can perform a multi-part piece for recording.

- Students have experience listening to recordings of multi-part music and analyzing the use of balance, pan, equalization, and effects processing in the recording.

## Procedures

1. Help students, as a group, generate specific criteria for making critical evaluations of the quality of recorded performances. Explain that the criteria should focus on the use of balance, pan, equalization, and effects processing. Encourage them to cite specific examples of good and bad recordings, according to these criteria, with which they are familiar.

2. Have students design an evaluation form that includes the criteria, as well as scales for rating how effectively various recordings meet the criteria (extremely well, very well, well, fairly, poorly).

3. Record an ensemble performance on four or more tracks, each at an optimum record level.

4. Have students listen to the recording and analyze its effectiveness using the evaluation form. Encourage them to discuss and explain the reasons for their ratings.

5. Help students make adjustments to the balance, pan, equalization, and effects processing of each track to improve the recording according to the results of the evaluation.

6. Ask students to record their final mix to stereo cassette for later comparison, evaluation, or broadcast.

## Indicators of Success

- Students develop criteria for evaluating balance, pan, equalization, and effects processing in a multi-track recording of a live performance.

- Students apply criteria they have developed and adjust the recording tracks to enhance the original recording.

## Follow-up

- Discuss with students the accuracy of the evaluation form developed in the Procedures. Have them generate suggestions to revise the form and then use it for evaluating other recordings.

# STANDARD 7B

*Proficient*

***Evaluating music and music performances:*** *Students evaluate a performance, composition, arrangement, or improvisation by comparing it to similar or exemplary models.*

## Objective

- Students will evaluate their own and others' compositions by comparing the compositions to an exemplary student composition.

## Materials

- Computers connected to General MIDI keyboards with powered speakers or headphones

- Completed student compositions produced with sequencing, notation, accompaniment, or digital audio software

- Sequencing, notation, accompaniment, or digital audio software, as needed to play completed student compositions

- Word processing software

- Recording of an exemplary student composition

## Prior Knowledge and Experiences

- Students have basic word processing skills.

## Procedures

1. Explain to students that we often evaluate compositions in terms of how they compare to compositions that we consider exemplary. Discuss the characteristics of an exemplary composition.

2. Play the recording of an exemplary student composition. Lead a discussion about what makes this composition especially effective. Have students make a list of criteria that describe the strengths of the composition—for example, the melody is well-crafted, the rhythms are unified yet varied; the chords or accompaniment fit well with the melody; the instruments or voices are well-blended and balanced; or the overall composition is interesting, imaginative, fresh, or intriguing.

3. Have students each select a composition that they completed earlier and that they consider an example of their best work. Pair students and have them listen to each other's compositions. Have students describe for each other the strengths and weaknesses of their compositions by comparing them to the exemplary composition, referring to the criteria developed in step 2.

4. Have students use word processing software to write an openended description and evaluation of their own compositions, again comparing their compositions to the exemplary composition.

## Indicators of Success

- Students write an open-ended narrative evaluating their own compositions by comparing them to an exemplary student composition.

## Follow-up

- To prepare for a concert of the students' original compositions, have students revise and extend the evaluations they wrote in the Procedures into program notes for a printed concert program.

# STANDARD 8B

***Understanding relationships between music, the other arts, and disciplines outside the arts:*** *Students compare characteristics of two or more arts within a particular historical period or style and cite examples from various cultures.*

## Objective

- Students will create a multimedia presentation about music, visual art, and dance or theatre of a particular historical period.

## Materials

- Computers that have Internet access and General MIDI sound generation (internal sound card— Windows; QuickTime Musical Instruments— Macintosh) connected to powered speakers or headphones

- Multimedia software such as *HyperStudio* (Torrance, CA: Knowledge Adventure), *PowerPoint* (Redmond, WA: Microsoft Corporation), or *AppleWorks* (Cupertino, CA: Apple Computer)

- Web browser software such as *Netscape Communicator* (Mountain View, CA: Netscape) or *Internet Explorer* (Redmond, WA: Microsoft Corporation)

- Collection of CDs

- Computer display projector and screen (optional)

- Copies of handout containing short descriptions of periods in music history

- Copies of handout with teacher guidelines for creating multimedia presentations (see page 142)

## Prior Knowledge and Experiences

- Students have experience using the selelcted multimedia software.

- Students know how to search the Internet and download files.

## Procedures

1. Distribute handouts on music history and with guidelines for creating multimedia presentations. Explain any unfamiliar terminology.

2. Divide the class into groups and ask each group to choose a historical period to research. Explain that for their research, they should browse the Internet, listen to CDs, and create multimedia projects. [*Note:* Project development may take up to four weeks.]

3. Have the groups present their projects and evaluate how effectively they related music of the selected historical period to other arts of that time. At the end of each presentation, ask the class questions to assess their learning.

## Indicators of Success

- Students identify important creations in music, visual arts, and either dance or theatre of a selected historical period.

- Students compare characteristics of the arts in their multimedia projects and relate them to events in the selected period in history.

## Follow-up

- Have students collaborate to draw a timeline showing dates of artists in each of the selected arts, as well as styles in each of the arts, for each historical period.

*(continued)*

# Guidelines for Creating Multimedia Presentations

1. Choose a specific period in musical history (Renaissance, Baroque, Classical, Romantic, or Twentieth Century).

2. Create a multimedia product that details important artistic creations in music and visual art, as well as either dance or theatre, of that period in history.

3. Relate the innovations in each of these arts and state any possible connections between them. Describe and compare characteristics of the selected arts of that period.

4. Include the following audiovisual aids: music examples on a CD, pictures of art and architecture of that particular period in history, and video clips of relevant information.

5. Include a screen that gives a detailed time line of world history during that particular period.

6. Include buttons that show connections between all of the disciplines featured.

7. Include a card at the end of the project that asks questions about the connections made in the presentation.

8. At the end of the project, share stacks with other students in the class.

# STANDARD 8C

*Proficient*

***Understanding relationships between music, the other arts, and disciplines outside the arts:*** *Students explain ways in which the principles and subject matter of various disciplines outside the arts are interrelated with those of music.*

## Objective

- Students will compare manifestations of fractals in mathematics, visual arts, and music.

## Materials

- Computers that have Internet access and General MIDI sound generation (internal sound card— Windows; QuickTime Musical Instruments— Macintosh) connected to powered speakers or headphones

- Web browser software such as *Netscape Communicator* (Mountain View, CA: Netscape) or *Internet Explorer* (Redmond, WA: Microsoft Corporation)

- Web browser prepared with bookmarks for fractal sites (see Fractal Web Sites on page 144)

- Software application for generating fractal-generated musical examples such as *A Musical Generator 2.0* (http://www.musoft-builders.com/index.shtml) or one of the various software applications listed on the Fractal Music Lab (http://www.fractal-musiclab.com/)

- Copies of teacher-prepared handout (see Fractal Web Sites on page 144)

## Procedures

1. Distribute the handout with the questions below. Play fractal music compositions from the Internet in the background as students use bookmarked web sites to answer the questions.

   (a) What are fractals? (geometric shapes that can be divided into copies of the whole)

   (b) Explain the aesthetic impulse that inspires artists to use fractals for creating works of art. (Similarity to self creates unity.)

   (c) Describe the main organizational principle you observe in pieces of fractal visual art. (repetition)

2. Lead students in a discussion of the relationships between math (geometry, proportion, etc.) and the arts. Emphasize the use of perspective, balance, simple addition, and related concepts used by artists in the creation of a work of art.

3. Play several minutes of the output of a fractal music generator, explaining that students are hearing a musical representation of fractals.

4. Demonstrate the interface of the fractal music generator. Explain which musical parameters are controlled by which aspects of the interface. Demonstrate how to save the output of the program as a MIDI file.

5. Tell students to explore the fractal-generating software and select the parameters that produce the most aesthetically interesting results. Have them save a sample output generated by the program, configured with their preferred settings.

6. Play selected examples of student work. Discuss the differences and similarities between the files. Have students articulate how their choices of parameters influenced the audible differences of the musical files.

7. Have students discuss the similarities in the visual art works studied and the music they created using the software.

*(continued)*

- Examples of fractal-generated music (see URLs for Examples of Fractal-Generated Music sidebar)

## Prior Knowledge and Experiences

- Students have studied fractals in their math class.

## Indicators of Success

- Students identify and discuss the representation of fractals in music, visual arts, and math.
- Students identify and discuss the aesthetic considerations that lead an artist to create works of art with the aid of mathematical systems.

## Follow-up

- Have students edit the files they created in the Procedures to shape their works into pieces with beginnings, middles, and ends. Then have them create a slide show combining their music with fractal-influenced visual images, using multimedia software such as *HyperStudio* (Torrance, CA: Knowledge Adventure), *PowerPoint* (Redmond, WA: Microsoft Corporation), or *AppleWorks* (Cupertino, CA: Apple Computer).

---

### Fractal Web Sites

- Fractal Faq (http://www.faqs.org/faqs/fractal-faq)
- The Fractal Microscope (http://www.ncsa.uiuc.edu/Edu/Fractal/Fractal_Home.html)
- Gallery of Fractal Images (http://graffiti.u-bordeaux.fr/MAPBX/roussel/)

---

### URLs for Examples of Fractal-Generated Music

- Composer David Clark Little's web page (http://www.sca.ahk.nl/david/index.html)
- Fractal Music Lab (http://www.fractalmusiclab.com)
- Composer Gary Lee Nelson's web page (http://www.timara.oberlin.edu/~gnelson/gnelson.htm)
- Fractal Vibes, by Phil Jackson (http://www.fractal-vibes.com/fvc/fractals.html)

# STANDARD 8C

***Understanding relationships between music, the other arts, and disciplines outside the arts:*** *Students explain ways in which the principles and subject matter of various disciplines outside the arts are interrelated with those of music.*

## Objective

- Students will create a commercial, including a script and music, and describe how they used musical principles to convey particular images or feelings.

## Materials

- (For each student or pair of students) Computers that have Internet access (optional) and microphones, connected to General MIDI keyboards and with powered speakers or headphones

- Sequencing software with digital audio such as *Cakewalk Home Studio* (Cambridge, MA: Cakewalk), *Metro 5* (Cambridge, MA: Cakewalk), or *MicroLogic AV* (Grass Valley, CA: Emagic Soft- und Hardware GmbH/Emagic, Inc.); or four-track tape recorder

- CD-ROM burner and appropriate software; or audiocassette player, DAT recorder, or MiniDisc recorder

## Prior Knowledge and Experiences

- Students have listened to examples of commercials and discussed how musical ideas were used to enhance the scripts.

- Students have a working knowledge of audio and sequencing equipment, as well as of sequencing software.

## Procedures

1. Divide the class into groups, or have students work individually, and have each group or individual identify a product or service, as well as a target audience. Explain that each group or individual should create a script for a commercial for the identified target audience.

2. Instruct students to record their scripts (narration) into sequencing software with digital audio or onto a four-track tape.

3. Have students play back their scripts so that the class can brainstorm musical ideas to enhance their scripts.

4. Tell students to sequence a musical background from brainstormed ideas and MIDI files from Internet. Explain that they should mix music and script, adjust EQ, add effects, and mix to stereo tracks.

5. Ask students to burn stereo recordings of their commercials onto an audio CD or record them to tape or disk.

6. Discuss with students how they used their knowledge of the principles of music to convey the images or feelings described in their scripts.

## Indicators of Success

- Students create clear and concise commercial scripts with music that enhances the message of each commercial.

- Students explain how they used their knowledge of the principles of music to convey the images or feelings described in their scripts.

## Follow-up

- Have the groups evaluate each other's commercials using a rubric based on the guidelines for the project.

# STANDARD 8D

## *Advanced*

*Understanding relationships between music, the other arts, and disciplines outside the arts:* Students compare the uses of characteristic elements, artistic processes, and organizational principles among the arts in different historical periods and different cultures.

## Objective

- Students will compose music to enhance film clips, demonstrating how the elements, process, and principles of music and film complement each other.

## Materials

- (For each student or pair of students) Computers with microphones, video-in capability, connected to General MIDI keyboards, with powered speakers or headphones

- Sequencing software such as *Musicshop* (Nashville: Opcode Systems) or *Cakewalk Home Studio* (Cambridge, MA: Cakewalk)

- Video-editing software such as *Adobe Premiere* (San Jose, CA: Adobe Systems) or *Avid Cinema* (Tewksbury, MA: Avid Technology)

- VHS tape recorder

## Prior Knowledge and Experiences

- Students have listened to and analyzed many different types of films, identifying aspects of music that enhance the films.

- Students can use cue sheets and identify hit points (highlighted events) in a film.

- Students have experience using sequencing and video-editing software.

## Procedures

1. Have students select a short section of a motion picture or TV show, such as the opening credits, and digitize this video clip.

2. Ask students to review the clip, chart hit points, and complete a cue sheet.

3. Direct students to sequence musical ideas for the hit points.

4. Have students import the MIDI sequence into the video-editing software to synchronize it with the film clip.

5. Tell students to print the finished product to videotape.

6. Discuss with students how the elements, processes, and organizational principles of music compare to those of film.

## Indicators of Success

- Students create music that is the same length as the film clip and that brings out the mood of the clip, and they synchronize the hits.

- Students use numerous musical components to build tension or relaxation, and they use special effects to enhance video.

- Students compare the elements, processes, and organizational principles of music and film.

## Follow-up

- Have students evaluate each other's videotapes, using a rubric based on the guidelines for the project.

# STANDARD 9B

*Proficient*

***Understanding music in relation to history and culture:*** *Students identify sources of American music genres, trace the evolution of those genres, and cite well-known musicians associated with them.*

## Objective

- Students will create and present a multimedia project based on their research and analysis of information about the effect of the social, cultural, and political influences on American popular music from 1950 to the present.

## Materials

- Computers with CD- or DVD-ROM player connected to powered speakers or headphones

- Multimedia software such as *HyperStudio* (Torrance, CA: Knowledge Adventure), *PowerPoint* (Redmond, WA: Microsoft Corporation), or *AppleWorks* (Cupertino, CA: Apple Computer)

- Variety of popular recordings from the 1950s to the present

- Copies of teacher-prepared handout containing information about what the unit will cover, including goals, objectives, assignments, and evaluation tools (rating scale)

- *Events That Changed the World* CD-ROM, developed by Robert Ingpen and Philip Wilkinson (Toronto: ICD Integrated Communications & Entertainment)

## Procedures

1. Distribute the handout and discuss the unit of study with students.

2. Divide the class into groups and assign each group to research a particular decade (from the 1950s to the present) and locate the following information: (a) popular styles of music; (b) popular musicians of the decade; (c) social and political issues of the decade; (d) song titles, CDs, or subjects of popular songs that reflect the social, political, and cultural trends of the decade.

3. Instruct students to create a visual display of their research—such as a chart, time line, or collage—that may be incorporated into the multimedia project.

4. Help students locate and share video and audio recordings of music that corresponds to their assigned decades.

5. Help students organize research, visuals, video, and audio demonstrating their understanding of the effects of social, cultural, and political influences on American popular music from 1950 to the present.

6. Ask each group to create a multimedia project using *HyperStudio*, including visuals, text, and music that reflects their research findings.

7. Have the groups present their projects to the class.

## Indicators of Success

- Students create and present multimedia projects that include popular styles of music and popular musicians of a selected decade.

- Students demonstrate their understanding of how the popular music and musicians of a selected decade were influenced by social and political issues of the decade.

*(continued)*

- *American History: Textbook for the Twenty-first Century* (New Rochelle, NY: MultiEducator)

- *Apple Pie Music* CD-ROM (Fairfield, CT: Queue)

- *The Instrumental History of Jazz* two-CD set, including enhanced CD, written by Willie L. Hill, Jr., compiled by Willie L. Hill, Jr., and Carl Griffin (International Association of Jazz Educators/N2K Encoded Jazz, 1997; available from MENC); or *The History of Jazz* software (Chicago: CLEARVUE/eav)

- Books and videos on American popular music from the 1950s to the present

## Prior Knowledge and Experiences

- Students have experience using the selected multimedia software.

## Follow-up

- Have students evaluate their projects created in the Procedures, using a rubric based on the guidelines for the project.

- Display the projects at a kiosk in the school.

# RESOURCES

## Software Referenced in This Text

### Accompaniment Software

*Band-in-a-Box.* Victoria, BC: PG Music.

*SmartMusic.* Eden Prairie, MN: Coda Music Technology.

*Visual Arranger.* Buena Vista, CA: Yamaha Corporation of America.

### Computer-Assisted Instruction Software

*American History: Textbook for the Twenty-first Century.* New Rochelle, NY: MultiEducator.

*Apple Pie Music.* Fairfield, CT: Queue.

*Dick Hyman's Century of Jazz Piano.* West New York, NJ: JSS Music, 1998.

*Events That Changed the World.* Developed by Robert Ingpen and Philip Wilkinson. Toronto: ICD Integrated Communications & Entertainment.

*The History of Jazz.* Chicago: Clearvue/eav.

*The Instrumental History of Jazz* by Willie L. Hill, Jr. Compiled by Willie L. Hill, Jr., and Carl Griffin. International Association of Jazz Educators/N2K Encoded Jazz. Available from MENC.

*Making More Music.* New York: Learn Technologies Interactive.

*Making Music.* New York: Learn Technologies Interactive.

*Music Ace.* Chicago: Harmonic Vision.

*Music Ace 2.* Chicago: Harmonic Vision.

*Music Lessons.* Northfield MN: MiBAC Music Software.

*Note Speller.* Champaign, IL: Electronic Courseware Systems.

*Practica Musica.* Kirkland, WA: Ars Nova Software.

*Rhythm Tutor.* Palo Alto, CA: Copperman Software Products.

*Rock Rap 'n Roll.* Reading, MA: Scott Foresman.

### Digital Audio Recording Software

*PeakLE.* Petaluma, CA: BIAS.

*Sound Forge XP.* Madison, WI: Sonic Foundry.

*SoundHandle* (freeware) by Dale Veeneman. Download from ZDNet (http://www.zdnet.com).

### Multimedia Software

*AppleWorks.* Cupertino, CA: Apple Computer.

*HyperStudio.* Torrance, CA: Knowledge Adventure.

*PowerPoint.* Redmond, WA: Microsoft Corporation.

### Notation Software

*Encore.* Philadelphia: GVOX.

*Finale.* Eden Prairie, MN: Coda Music Technology.

*Music Time.* Philadelphia: GVOX.

*Overture.* Cambridge, MA: Cakewalk.

*Print Music.* Eden Prairie, MN: Coda Music Technology.

*Sibelius.* Cambridge, England: The Sibelius Group.

### Page Layout Software

*AppleWorks.* Cupertino, CA: Apple Computer.

*Microsoft Word.* Redmond, WA: Microsoft Corporation.

*PageMaker.* San Jose, CA: Adobe Systems.

### Sequencing Software

*Cakewalk Home Studio.* Cambridge, MA: Cakewalk.

*Master Tracks Pro.* Philadelphia: GVOX.

*Musicshop.* Nashville: Opcode Systems.

### Sequencing Software with Digital Audio

*Cakewalk Home Studio.* Cambridge, MA: Cakewalk.

*Metro 5.* Cambridge, MA: Cakewalk.

*MicroLogic AV.* Grass Valley, CA: Emagic Soft- und Hardware GmbH/Emagic, Inc.

### Video Editing Software

*Adobe Premiere.* San Jose, CA: Adobe Systems.

*Avid Cinema.* Tewksbury, MA: Avid Technology.

### Video Teleconferencing Software

*CU-See-Me.* Nashua, NH: CUseeMe Networks.

*Microsoft Netmeeting.* Redmond, WA: Microsoft Corporation.

### Web Audio Software

*RealPlayer.* Seattle: RealNetworks.

### Web Page Authoring Software

*Microsoft Front Page Express.* Redmond, WA: Microsoft Corporation.

*Netscape Composer.* Mountain View, CA: Netscape.

### Web Browser Software

*Internet Explorer.* Redmond, WA: Microsoft Corporation.

*Netscape Communicator.* Mountain View, CA: Netscape.

*Netscape Navigator.* Mountain View, CA: Netscape.

### Word Processing and Office Software

*AppleWorks.* Cupertino, CA: Apple Computer.

*Microsoft Excel.* Redmond, WA: Microsoft Corporation.

*Microsoft Word.* Redmond, WA: Microsoft Corporation.

*Microsoft Works.* Redmond, WA: Microsoft Corporation.

*WordPerfect.* Ottawa: Corel Corporation.

## World Wide Web Sites Referenced in This Text

Amazon (http://www.amazon.com).

Ancient Future (http://www.ancient-future.com).

ArtCyclopedia (http://www.artcyclopedia.com).

ArtsEdge (http://artsedge.kennedy-center.org).

Blues Lines Using Guide Tones (http://www.music.sc.edu/Departments/Jazz/BluesGT.pdf).

Britannica.com (http://www.britannica.com).

CD Now (http://www.cdnow.com).

Classical Archives (http://www.prs.net).

Claude Debussy—The Musical Impressions (http://public.srce.hr/~fsupek/index.html).

David Clark Little's web page (http://www.sca.ahk.nl/david/index.html).

Duke Ellington: Celebrating 100 Years of the Man and His Music (www.dellington.org).

Filamentality (www.kn.pacbell.com).

Fractal Faq (http://www.faqs.org/faqs/fractal-faq).

The Fractal Microscope (http://www.ncsa.uiuc.edu/Edu/Fractal/Fractal_Home.html).

Fractal Music Lab (http://www.fractalmusiclab.com).

Fractal Vibes (by Phil Jackson) (http://www.fractal-vibes.com/fvc/fractals.html).

Gallery of Fractal Images (http://graffiti.u-bordeaux.fr/MAPBX/roussel/).

Gary Lee Nelson's web page (http://www.timara.oberlin.edu/~gnelson/gnelson.htm).

HyperHistory (http://www.hyperhistory.com/online_n2/History_n2/a.html).

Jazz in America (www.jazzinamerica.com).

John Philip Sousa (http://www.dws.org/sousa).

KIDiddles (http://www.kididdles.com).

The Music of John Philip Sousa (http://www.dws.org/sousa/music.htm).

A Musical Generator 2.0 (http://www.musoft-builders.com/index.shtml).

National Gallery of Art (http://www.nga.gov).

RootsWorld (http://www.rootsworld.com).

Sousa Archives for Band Research

(http://www.library.uiuc.edu/sousa).

The United States Marine Band—John Philip Sousa
(http://www.marineband.usmec.mil/edu_sousa.html).

WebQuest (http://edweb.sdsu.edu/webquest/).

Yahoo Groups (www.yahoo.com).

ZDNet (www.zdnet.com).

## Music Referenced in This Text

*Bach Chorale Standard MIDI Files.* Pacific, MO: Mel Bay. IBM
(95050IMD); Macintosh (95050MMD).

"The Cat Came Back," in *Share the Music,* Grade 4 (New York:
Macmillan/McGraw-Hill, 1995, 2000).

*English Folk-Song Fantasy* by Frank Erickson. Van Nuys, CA: Alfred
Publishing Company.

*English Folk Song Suite* by Ralph Vaughan Williams. New York:
Boosey & Hawkes. Level 4.

*Fantasy on a Canadian Folk Song* by Mike Hannickel. Lexington, KY:
Curnow Music Press.

"For the Beauty of the Earth" by John Rutter. Chapel Hill, NC:
Hinshaw Music. SATB. Level 3.

*The Hal Leonard Real Jazz Book.* Milwaukee: Hal Leonard
Corporation, 1997.

"Russian Sailors' Dance," from *The Red Poppy,* by Reinhold Glière,
arr. James Curnow. Milwaukee: Hal Leonard Corporation. Level 4.

*Tunes for Three—Treble Recorder,* arr. Keith Stent. Pacific, MO: Kevin
Mayhew Publishers/Mel Bay Publications, 1999.

"Variations on a Korean Folk Song" by John Barnes Chance. New
York: Boosey & Hawkes/Alfred Publishing Company. Level 4.

## Methods and Other Books Referenced in This Text

*Alligator Pie* by Dennis Lee and Frank Newfield. Toronto: Macmillan,
1974.

*Duke Ellington Education Kit, Beyond Category.* Parsippany, NJ: Dale
Seymour Publications/Pearson Learning, 1997.

*It's Snowing, It's Snowing* by Jack Prelutsky. New York: Greenwillow Books, 1984.

*Let Your Voice Be Heard: Songs from Ghana and Zimbabwe,* 2d ed., by Abraham Kobena Adzenyah, Dumisani Maraire, and Judith Cook Tucker. Danbury, CT: World Music Press, 1997.

*Tools for Powerful Student Evaluation* by Susan R. Farrell. Fort Lauderdale, FL: Meredith Music Publications, 1997.

## Audio Recordings Referenced in This Text

*Been in the Storm So Long: Spirituals, Folk Tales and Children's Games.* Smithsonian Folkways 40031.

*The Essential Count Basie, vol. 3.* Legacy/Sony Music VCK 44150.

*Hush.* Performed by Yo-Yo Ma and Bobby McFerrin. Sony CD SK48177.

*Jazz Sebastien Bach.* Performed by Swingle Singers. Philips 824 703-2.

*Take 6 Greatest Hits.* Warner 47375.

*Yardbird Suite—Ultimate Charlie Parker Collection.* WEA/Atlantic/Rhino 72260.

## Additional Resources

### Books

*Computers and the Music Educator, 4th ed.,* by David S. Mash. SoundTree Publications, Melville, NY, 1996.

*Experiencing Music Technology, 2nd ed.,* by David Williams and Peter Webster. Schirmer Books, New York, 1999.

*From Research to the Music Classroom: Applications of Research in Music Technology* by William L. Berz and Judith Bowman. Reston, VA: Music Educators National Conference, 1994.

*Jazz Improvisation Series Approaching the Standards,* vols. 1–3, by Willie L. Hill, Jr. Miami, FL: Warner Bros. Publications, 2000–

*Teaching Music with Technology* by Thomas E. Rudolph. GIA Publications. Chicago, 1996.

*Technology Strategies for Music Education* by Thomas Rudolph, Floyd

Richmond, David Mash, and David Williams. TI:ME
Publications, Wyncote, PA, 1997.

## Journals and Magazines

*Electronic Musician.*

*The Journal for Technology in Music Learning.*

*Keyboard Magazine*

## MENC Resources on Music and Arts Education Standards

*Aiming for Excellence: The Impact of the Standards Movement on Music Education.* 1996. #1012.

*Implementing the Arts Education Standards.* Set of five brochures: "What School Boards Can Do," "What School Administrators Can Do," "What State Education Agencies Can Do," "What Parents Can Do," "What the Arts Community Can Do." 1994. #4022. Each brochure is also available in packs of 20.

*National Standards for Arts Education: What Every Young American Should Know and Be Able to Do in the Arts.* 1994. #1605.

*Opportunity-to-Learn Standards for Arts Education.* 1995. #1643.

*Opportunity-to-Learn Standards for Music Instruction: Grades PreK–12.* 1994. #1619.

*Performing with Understanding: The Challenge of the National Standards for Music Education,* edited by Bennett Reimer. 2000. #1672.

*Performance Standards for Music: Strategies and Benchmarks for Assessing Progress toward the National Standards, Grades PreK–12.* 1996. #1633.

*Perspectives on Implementation: Arts Education Standards for America's Students.* 1994. #1622.

"Prekindergarten Music Education Standards" (brochure). 1995. #4015 (set of 10).

*The School Music Program—A New Vision: The K–12 National Standards, PreK Standards, and What They Mean to Music Educators.* 1994. #1618.

*Teaching Examples: Ideas for Music Educators.* 1994. #1620.

## MENC's *Strategies for Teaching* Series

*Strategies for Teaching Prekindergarten Music,* compiled and edited by Wendy L. Sims. #1644.

*Strategies for Teaching K–4 General Music,* compiled and edited by Sandra L. Stauffer and Jennifer Davidson. #1645.

*Strategies for Teaching Middle-Level General Music,* compiled and edited by June M. Hinckley and Suzanne M. Shull. #1646.

*Strategies for Teaching High School General Music,* compiled and edited by Keith P. Thompson and Gloria J. Kiester. #1647.

*Strategies for Teaching Elementary and Middle-Level Chorus,* compiled and edited by Ann Roberts Small and Judy K. Bowers. #1648.

*Strategies for Teaching High School Chorus,* compiled and edited by Randal Swiggum. #1649.

*Strategies for Teaching Strings and Orchestra,* compiled and edited by Dorothy A. Straub, Louis S. Bergonzi, and Anne C. Witt. #1652.

*Strategies for Teaching Middle-Level and High School Keyboard,* compiled and edited by Martha F. Hilley and Tommie Pardue. #1655.

*Strategies for Teaching Beginning and Intermediate Band,* compiled and edited by Edward J. Kvet and Janet M. Tweed. #1650.

*Strategies for Teaching High School Band,* compiled and edited by Edward J. Kvet and John E. Williamson. #1651.

*Strategies for Teaching Specialized Ensembles,* compiled and edited by Robert A. Cutietta. #1653.

*Strategies for Teaching Middle-Level and High School Guitar,* compiled and edited by William E. Purse, James L. Jordan, and Nancy Marsters. #1654.

*Strategies for Teaching: Technology,* compiled and edited by Sam Reese, Kimberly McCord, and Kimberly Walls. #1657.

*Strategies for Teaching: Guide for Music Methods Classes,* compiled and edited by Louis O. Hall with Nancy R. Boone, John Grashel, and Rosemary C. Watkins. #1656.

For more information on these and other MENC publications, write to or call MENC Publications Sales, 1806 Robert Fulton Drive, Reston, VA 20191-4348; 800-828-0229; or see the MENC web site (http://www.menc.org).

# OTHER TECHNOLOGY-BASED STRATEGIES

## IN THE *STRATEGIES FOR TEACHING* SERIES

### K–4 General Music

*Standard 5D, p. 45:* Using software to help students hear and identify pitches from the major scale.

### Middle-Level General Music

*Standard 3C, p. 24:* Using electronic keyboards to improvise over one-finger chords and built-in rhythms.

*Standard 9A, p. 54:* Using *Musical Instruments* CD-ROM to identify distinguishing characteristics of genres and styles.

### High School General Music

*Standard 4B, pp. 65–66:* Using notation software to arrange the melody of a Bach minuet.

*Standard 6C, pp. 78–79:* Using *Dvorak Symphony no. 9* CD-ROM to describe compositional structure.

*Standard 9E, p. 104:* Using the World Wide Web to research and listen to traditional and current Chinese music.

### Elementary and Middle-Level Chorus

*Standard 4C, Gr. 5–8, p. 97:* Using keyboards and synthesizers for nontraditional accompaniment.

### High School Band

*Standard 4D, p. 21:* Using notation software to create, notate, and perform melodies.

### Middle-Level and High School Guitar

*Standard 2C, High School, p. 42:* Using a sequencer to learn the parts for a four-part chorale.

### Middle and High School Keyboard

*Standard 4B, High School, p. 49:* Using keyboards to arrange a composition in four parts.

### Specialized Ensembles

*Standard 2C, Gr. 9–12 (guitar and electronic ensemble), pp. 16–17:* Practicing one part of a Bach chorale while a sequencer plays the other parts.

*Standard 4B, Gr. 9–12 (electronic ensemble), p. 51:* Using synthesizers to create a new arrangement for an existing piece.

*Standard 4B, Gr. 9–12 (electronic ensemble), pp. 52–53:* Arranging a Renaissance composition using combinations of synthesizer timbres.

*Standard 6B, Gr. 9–12 (electronic ensemble), p. 55:* Defining and exploring various types of signal processing in recorded examples.

*Standard 7A, Gr. 5–8 (Cuban percussion ensemble), pp. 84–85:* Using a sequencer to play a commercial sequence while students perform a percussion ensemble accompaniment.